ANNA

ANNA

DIANE SEBRA

GRANDIN BOOK COMPANY
OREM, UTAH

Copyright © 1994 Grandin Book Company

Grandin Book Company
1170 North Industrial Park Drive, Orem, Utah 84057
All rights reserved. International copyright secured.
Copying or reproducing this publication in whole or part is
subject to penalty under Federal Copyright Law.

ISBN 0-910523-43-6

For my loving husband, Tim,
and for Jeanne Lewis,
who was my inspiration,
coach, and friend.

CHAPTER 1

"ANNA!" Emily yelled to her daughter from the kitchen. "Dinner is almost ready, so get cleaned up!"

Anna glanced over at her two friends, who were lying on her bed watching MTV. Sting was crooning his heart out on stage.

"Do you guys want to stay for dinner?"

Connie, who was always interested in food, spoke up. "Well, what are you having?"

Anna smiled at her. "Does it matter?"

"Heck yeah, it matters! If you're having chicken, I'm all yours. If you're serving up liver and ketchup, I'm outta here!"

Rebecca snickered. "Gosh, Connie!"

"What? Don't tell me you would stay for liver."

"No, but I wouldn't tell them that's why I wasn't staying!"

All three girls started to giggle together.

"Okay, hold on just a second." Anna turned and yelled down the hallway, "Mom! What are we having?"

"Enchilada casserole!" was the response from the kitchen.

Anna looked inquisitively at Connie. "Will that suit your needs?"

"I don't know. Can I call my mom to see what we are having?"

Rebecca gaped at Connie in disbelief.

"Oh, close your trap, Becs. I was just joking."

Rebecca's cheeks turned a light shade of pink as she stuck her tongue out at Connie.

Anna turned and hollered back down the hallway, "Mom! Can Rebecca and Connie eat over?"

Emily poked her head in the doorway. "You don't need to yell, dear. And I already figured they would be staying. Do you like enchilada casserole, Connie?"

Now it was Connie's turn to blush. "Yes, Sister Harmon. It sounds great."

Anna and Rebecca hee-hawed with laughter.

"You girls are silly. Anna? Would you like some help down the hallway?"

"Yes, please."

Emily positioned herself behind her daughter, unlocked the rear wheels, and pushed her wheelchair towards the dining room.

"SO, WHAT DO you girls have planned for tonight? Anything exciting?"

"As a matter of fact, Brother Harmon, there is a dance at the Stake Center. Connie and I were trying to talk Anna into going."

Gary Harmon's smile froze on his face. He dropped his gaze to his plate.

"Oh, by the way, Anna" Connie interjected, "did we mention that Brian Dailey would be there?"

Anna flashed her a threatening look.

"Ooohhh! Anna has a boyfriend! Anna has a boyfriend!" Jason Harmon taunted his older sister.

"Be quiet, cretin."

"Anna!" Emily snapped. "Apologize to your brother."

"But Mom . . . ," Anna started.

"Now, young lady."

Anna sighed heavily. "Sorry, little rodent."

Jason giggled and Emily rolled her eyes. "What am I going to do with you two?"

They ate in silence for a while, the only noise being the occasional clang of a fork connecting with a plate. Anna felt grateful that for the moment the pressure of going to the youth dance had been lifted. And she unknowingly shared her relief with her father. It broke his heart to know that he made Anna's participation in normal youth activities difficult. If only it had been him instead of his beautiful daughter.

"Anyone care for dessert? I made apple crunch!"

A unanimous decision sent Emily into the kitchen for warm apple crunch and vanilla ice cream.

"So, Anna, are you coming to the dance with us or what?"

Gary stood up so quickly that he almost tipped his chair over backwards. "Excuse me everyone. I think I'll go help my wife in the kitchen." He left the room as abruptly as he had stood up. Rebecca flinched and looked at Anna.

"Is it something we said?"

Anna just shrugged. "I don't think so."

"You know, Anna," Connie chimed in, "you have a terrific way of avoiding a question."

"That's true!" Rebecca agreed.

Anna looked innocently from one to the other. "What question?"

"The dance!" Rebecca practically screamed. "Are you going to the dance!"

"Oh! That question!" Anna chuckled. "Well, buds, sorry to disappoint you, but I think I'll sit this one out, no pun intended. There's a good movie on tonight, and . . . I have some reading to catch up on for . . . my history class." Both Connie and Rebecca eyed her suspiciously.

"Are you sure?" Connie asked, "Even though Brian will be there?"

Anna's eyes bulged and she motioned towards Jason, who for once had been sitting quietly and taking it all in. "Not in front of the kid!"

"I'm not a kid!" Jason insisted defiantly.

"Well, if you're not a kid, then you are the shortest adult I've ever seen!" Connie chirped. Jason stuck his tongue out at her and ran for the kitchen. "Okay, your whole family is gone. We could have so much fun at the dance, Anna. And who knows, maybe tonight will be the night that Brian notices you!"

Anna sneered at Connie. "Ha, ha. Very funny."

"You know, Anna, in a way she's right. Not about him noticing your existence, but about how tonight could be the night. This could be your opportunity to let him know you are interested."

For a moment, Anna actually let herself consider this, then came to her senses and dismissed the idea completely. "That's totally ridiculous and you guys know it. Why would a guy like Brian want a girl like me?"

Rebecca looked at her best friend, knowing full well what the answer to her next question would be, but she asked it anyway. "What do you mean 'a girl like you'? Anna, you are beautiful, intelligent, and you have a great sense of humor."

The look Anna gave her said it all, but she chose to verbalize it as well. "Rebecca, don't play dumb. You know very well that I meant a girl in a wheelchair."

"If that's all he sees when he looks at you, then he doesn't deserve you."

Anna sighed at this. She had often heard the same argument from her parents, but it didn't change the fact that guys were not exactly beating down the door. "Look, I know you guys mean well, but I am really kind of tired. So thanks anyway, but I'm just gonna hang out at home tonight."

"Well then, we're not going either. We'll stay here with you," Rebecca stated.

Connie looked at Rebecca as if she were crazy. Rebecca only smiled back at her. "Isn't that right, Connie?"

"Uh . . . yeah, sure. That's right."

"No, no. You guys don't have to stay here. Go to the dance and have a great time."

"You heard her, Becs! Let's go get ready!"

Rebecca glared at Connie. "We can't just eat and run. That's rude!"

"Yeah, don't go yet. You still have two hours before it starts. Besides, you haven't had dessert yet."

Connie immediately brightened up. "Oh, yeah!" she cried excitedly. "How could I forget?!"

Rebecca and Anna looked at each other and laughed.

"Can you believe it, Becs?" Anna chuckled. "Connie forgot dessert! I guess there really is a first time for everything!"

CHAPTER 2

Sunday, April 30

Dear Diary,

Well, I managed to get out of another dance last night. Rebecca and Connie tried their best to get me to go, but I told them the one about the good movie on television. Then I threw in being tired just for good measure. They actually thought that telling me Brian would be there would change my mind. Don't they realize that seeing him dance with all those other girls would just kill me? I wouldn't be able to stand it! I would never and will never intentionally put myself through that kind of misery.

Today at Sunday School I arrived a little early so I could get to the back of the room without disturbing anyone. And guess what happened! Brian sat down right in front of me! It was so cool! He was wearing that khaki shirt I love—the one that makes him look so tan. Connie told me to drop my pencil by his foot so he would have to turn around and talk to me, but I couldn't get up the nerve. I just stared at the back of his head the whole time.

I guess I should write something spiritual now. Today at church we had analogies coming out of our ears. First, in Sunday School, we had a lesson about how the Father, Son, and Holy Ghost all work together. Our teacher brought out a three-legged stool made out of construction paper. He said that each leg represented one member of the Godhead. The stool stood fine with all three legs, but each time he took away just one leg the stool fell over. Thus, the Godhead can only function with all three members. Then in Young Women's, our lesson was on testimonies. My advisor brought out a pitcher that was half full of Kool-Aid. The pitcher represented us, and the Kool-Aid was our testimony. She explained that without effort on our part, our testimony would just sit as it was. Then she held up a small rock which she called "daily prayer," then dropped it in the pitcher. She dropped in three more rocks called "daily scripture reading," "fasting," and "church attendance." Each time she dropped in another rock, the Kool-Aid rose. She did this until it was all the way up to the top. She finished by explaining that when we obey the commandments, we nurture our testimonies.

"ARE YOU WRITING in your journal again?" Jason plopped down on the foot of Anna's bed.

"Yeah. What do you want, squirt?"

"You're just trying to be like Doogie Howser, writing your journal on a computer."

"Jason, what do you want?"

When he got up and stood over her shoulder to read what she had written, she quickly dimmed the screen. "Mom said it's time for dinner, so come on."

"Fine. I'll be there in a minute. Leave."

"You're a jerk, Anna!" He turned and strutted out of the room.

Anna brought her screen back up and thought for a moment.

Well, it's time to go for dinner. Jason, the rug rat, is getting so big. He must have grown at least a foot over the past couple of months.

Gotta go . . .
The Church is true . . .
Anna

She saved her text and logged off her computer.

CHAPTER 3

ANNA rolled into her fifth period art class just as she had her Sunday School class, a little early so as not to disturb anyone. But this was not the only reason she arrived before anyone else; she had art class with Brian. And because his desk was all the way on the other side of the room, her only clear view of him was when he first walked in.

"Hi, Anna! How are you today?"

"Howdy, Mrs. Peterson. I'm fine, thanks."

"Today we will continue to work on our magazine pictures, so if you would like to begin working early, that would be fine."

Anna quickly rolled across the room to her cubby hole where she kept her art supplies. She wanted desperately to get back to her table before anyone arrived. For some reason it embarrassed her terribly to move past other students in the classroom. She was fine anywhere else, but the classroom was her one downfall. It humiliated her beyond words to bump someone with her wheelchair.

She piled her supplies on her lap and headed back to the safe haven of her table. She was just reaching the corner of the table when the first students came bursting through the door.

The magazine picture assignment required quite a bit of creativity. Each student had to find a black and white picture in a magazine, preferably one with a lot of activity. Once you found the perfect picture, you cut out just a small piece in any shape from anywhere on the page. Then you glued your small little piece onto a white sheet of paper. You could turn your little magazine picture any direction when you glued it. Next you had to create a new picture around your piece of magazine, using as much of the white piece of paper as you possibly could. The idea was to use your imagination to change one picture into another.

The magazine picture Anna cut out was of a little boy's elbow and forearm. Behind his arm was some water splashing up from a fountain. From this picture she was creating was a very pathetic looking ostrich. Well, Anna knew it was an ostrich, since she was the one who was drawing it. But the general public would not recognize it as such. It actually looked more like some weird muppet animal. Anna was so embarrassed at how poorly her picture was turning out that every time another student would walk by, Anna would find some reason to either turn her picture over or plop something big on top of it.

This picture will be a secret between me and Mrs. Peterson! Anna thought, at least she did until the end of class.

"Listen up, students!" Mrs. Peterson announced. "We have a little twist on our current project. If you've already put your name on it, take it off. If you haven't, please leave it that way. I will give you two more days to finish your projects. On the third day, we will place all of your pictures along the back wall. Your fellow students will walk around and silently grade each picture. At the end of class I will gather everyone's list of grades. The grade you receive for your artwork will be an average of what your classmates give you. And remember, I want all of your pictures turned in by the end of class on Wednesday. Not turning in a project will merit an automatic 'F.'"

Oh, great! Anna thought. My worst project of the year, and Mrs. Peterson decides to have a mass critique! I don't know what's worse, an "F" or total humiliation. I have about a "B+" average now, so an "F" would drop me down to about a "C." I don't really want a "C," and I guess if my name won't be on top of it . . . I suppose it won't be too bad. I just hope no one has seen it on my desk!

Brian's supply cubbyhole was two spaces away from her own, and one day before anyone else arrived, Anna had snuck a peek at his picture. When she pulled it out of his storage space, she couldn't believe her eyes! His picture was incredible! It took her a few moments to even find the little piece of magazine. Around that little scrap, Brian had drawn the most perfect diamond-back rattlesnake she had ever seen. His picture took up every single inch of the paper.

This is fabulous! she thought. He is so talented. He's sure to get an "A." She then looked down at her own pitiful attempt at art. On second thought, maybe I'll play sick on Wednesday. I'll still turn in my picture on Tuesday, but no one can make me watch others grade it!

"ARE YOU READY to go, Anna?" Emily Harmon called to her daughter from the car. "Sister Tibble and Sister Carson will be at the house in 20 minutes."

Today was Monday, which meant two sisters from the Relief Society were coming to help Anna exercise. The doctor who treated her after the accident recommended that she do leg exercises three days a week to keep her legs strong and toned. When the Relief Society presidency heard this, they volunteered to have two sisters help Anna exercise every Monday, Wednesday, and Friday afternoon.

"Yeah, Mom, I'm ready. I just need to stop by my locker for a second. Is it okay if Connie and Becca come along?"

"Of course. But hurry up!"

They arrived home just minutes before the Relief Society sisters got there.

"Anna!" Connie giggled, looking out the front window at the women getting out of their car. "It's not Sister Tibble and Sister Carson; it's Brian's mom and sister!"

"No way!" Anna flushed a deep red.

"Your future mother and sister-in-law are coming to help you exercise!" Rebecca chimed in.

"Oh, you guys," Anna said, "I can never decide if it's a good thing or a bad thing when they come."

Rebecca got up to peek out the window with Connie. "Of course it's good," she responded. "A guy's mom is a great ally to have when it's time to start dating."

All three girls were giggling when the Daileys reached the front door.

"Anna," Connie chuckled, "it's for you!"

As Sister Dailey guided Anna through her second set of leg lifts, Anna asked, "So, uh . . . Sister Dailey? What happened to Sister Tibble and Sister Carson?"

"Well, Sister Tibble ended up baby-sitting her granddaughter. When Sister Carson called to ask me to fill in, I told her that my daughter and I could simply come together. So I just left a note for Brian asking him to prepare dinner."

Just the mention of his name sent Anna's heart racing. She felt her cheeks get hot and turned her head before Sister Dailey could notice. "Oh, I didn't know Brian could cook."

"Sure! My little Brian is a great cook!"

Connie snorted from the corner where she was sitting. "Sounds like he'll make someone a great husband!"

Anna flashed her a horrified look.

"I believe he will," Sister Dailey agreed.

Anna decided this conversation was getting out of hand. "Hey, Becs, do you and Connie want to stay for family home evening?"

Connie jumped in before Rebecca could even open her mouth. "Well, I don't know about old Becs, but I want to know what the snack will be!"

Anna and the Daileys laughed while Rebecca just looked appalled. "Connie!" she exclaimed wildly.

"Oh, relax, Becca darlin'. Everyone knows I was just joking!"

Rebecca's cheeks turned a light pink. "Well, I never know with you."

"Connie, I think my mom made brownies this morning, so we'll either have that or ice cream. Or maybe both."

Rebecca cracked a smile. "That sounds good. I love your mom's brownies. I'm staying!"

Now it was Connie's turn to look appallingly at Rebecca. "Why, Becs! I do believe I'm rubbing off on you! How shallow you've become!" Connie let out a cackle and thumped Rebecca on the back.

"Ha, ha. Laugh if you must," Rebecca replied. "But I know you love me, and you would probably keel over from boredom if I weren't around."

Connie put on her most sentimental expression. "It's true, Becs. You are the wind beneath my wings. Did you ever know that you're my hero?"

Rebecca smiled wildly. "It must have been cold there in my shadow!"

Anna slapped her forehead and laughed. "Really, Sister Dailey, these guys are not normally this mental."

"Sure we are!" Connie laughed. "We're even holding back some!"

"Well, you girls just carry on like normal. Our time is up anyway. I don't know who will be here on Wednesday. You never know, we may even come again."

"Oh, well, that would be fine," Anna said, as she threw Connie a glance that said, *Don't you dare say a word!*

CHAPTER 4

Sunday, May 14

Dear Diary,

I can't believe it's been two weeks since I've written! The past six days have been quite busy. Everything's churning around in my head, threatening to explode.
　I guess the best place to start would be last Monday. We got a letter from Troy. Since we got it on Monday, Dad decided to center family home evening around it. We invited Troy's friend, Amber, over also. We figured that if we got a letter, she probably got one as well, so Dad asked her to bring it with her and read it, if it wasn't too mushy. It was really great to hear how well his mission is going. He says that Venezuela is really hot and humid. But he loves the work he's doing and loves the people of Venezuela, so that makes weather easier to bear.
　Moving right along, on Wednesday my art teacher let other students grade our latest projects. Brian's is sure to get an "A." My own project was the worst I've done yet, but at least it wasn't the worst one there! I almost didn't turn it in, which would have given me an automatic "F." But I'm glad I did because I got a "C+." Now my grade won't drop too much.
　On Friday night Connie, Becs, and I hung out at the mall. Nothing too interesting happened. It was just a normal night filled with people watching.

But the last thing I have to write about is by far the best. As you probably guessed, it involves Brian. Nothing really spectacular, but a lot more than has ever happened before! It was last Saturday, and the youth had planned an activity for Santa Cruz Beach. Everything was fine until we got to the very edge of the sand. Connie and Rebecca thought that they would be able to push my chair across the sand. We got about three feet before they almost dumped me over on my face! My chair wedged in the sand, and they couldn't push or pull me out. Becca was just about to run and find Brother Ellis, when Brian and Karl Tanner strolled by. They told Becca not to bother Brother Ellis, because they would be able to get me out. I was so embarrassed! Each grabbed one handle of the chair, whipped me around backwards so that my back was to the ocean, and then they tilted my chair back so that all I could see was the sky! I wanted to crawl under a rock and die! Brian was actually pulling my chair! I never thought I'd see the day. Because of the way they were holding my chair, I was practically lying flat on the ground. And if I tilted my head back I could see Brian's face perfectly. Of course, I would also be looking straight up his nose, but any part of Brian is wonderful! Well, they got me to the water's edge without tipping me over, and the activity itself was a blast! We barbecued hotdogs and roasted marshmallows, played frisbee and football, and some brave souls even dared to boogieboard in the cold Pacific Ocean. Naturally, my Brian was one of those brave souls. At the end of the party, Karl and Brian got me back to the parking lot the same way they got me in. Both smelled like salt water and campfire smoke. Unfortunately, we rode in different cars. It may not sound like much of an interaction, but it was certainly better than nothing! Tonight is a regional fireside. I hope he goes!

The Church is true . . .
Anna

CHAPTER 5

"ANNA! Let's go! Your father is already out in the car!"

She gave her hair one last brush stroke, straightened her ribbon, and headed for the front door. *I really hope Brian will be at this fireside tonight!* she thought.

"Have a good time, dear. And remember who you are."

Anna rolled her eyes. "I know, Mom; I'm a daughter of God and an example to those around me."

Emily opened the door for her daughter. "Really, Anna. There is no need for such acerbity."

Anna looked back at her mom and laughed. "Acerbity? What the heck does that mean?"

"It means that you are being sarcastic to your mother. Now get going—your father is waiting."

Gary carefully lifted his daughter out of the car.

"Thanks for the ride, Dad. The fireside should be over around nine o'clock."

"I'll be here. Bye, sweetheart."

Anna rolled to the back of the chapel, where she had agreed to meet Connie and Rebecca. She slowly scanned the faces and backs of heads of those already there, looking for a particular boy with blond hair. She scoured the room three times but was disappointed when she didn't spot him or her friends.

"Hi, Anna." She turned to see who had greeted her with such a deep voice. As soon as she saw him, her cheeks grew hot and her heart raced.

"Hi, Brian."

"Are you here alone, also?"

If I were, would you marry me? Anna thought to herself and almost giggled out loud. "Well, Connie and Rebecca are supposed to meet me here, but they haven't shown up yet."

"Would it be okay if I sit with you? None of my friends are coming."

Oh, yes, Brian! Of course I'll marry you! She felt her throat closing and cleared it quickly. "Uh, yeah. Sure. That would be great."

"Great." Brian walked around behind her chair and took hold of the handgrips. "Well mi'lady, would you prefer the front, middle, or back?"

"Oh, let's go to the back, that way I can spot my friends when they come in." *And they will be sure to spot me with you!* Anna thought deviously.

"The back it is." He pushed her over to the second row from the back, on the right side of the chapel. "Will this pew do?"

"Yes, it's fine."

He parked her by the edge of the pew, then squeezed past her and sat down.

This is going to be some fireside! Anna was deliriously happy. She knew that with Brian sitting so close, she wouldn't be able to concentrate on what the speakers were saying. But she would make that sacrifice bravely and without complaint. *I'll impress him with intelligent and witty conversation,* she thought, *woo him with my irresistible charm, then capture his heart with my knowledge of things both worldly and spiritual. He doesn't stand a chance!*

Anna looked back at the door in time to see Connie and Rebecca come into the chapel. She watched them as they quickly scanned the room, looking for her chair no doubt. They spotted her and started towards her pew. Suddenly, Rebecca stopped dead, pointed at Anna, and whispered something to Connie. Connie now looked harder, realized what Rebecca had seen, then grinned from ear to ear. For some reason, Anna was now overcome with a sense of dread.

Please don't let Connie embarrass me! I know I can trust Becs to keep her mouth shut, but Connie is another story.

"Well, well. Hello, Anna. And hello to you, Brian."

Anna's cheeks immediately turned red. She glared at Connie and gave Rebecca a look, pleading to help keep Connie under control. However, Brian spoke before Rebecca had a chance.

"Hi, guys. I hope you don't mind me sitting with you. None of my friends wanted to come tonight, so I would have been a loner if Anna hadn't let me sit here."

Connie raised her eyebrows and smiled. "Oh, I'm sure Anna would never have allowed that to happen." Anna shot Connie a look that would have silenced anyone—anyone but Connie, of course. "And by the way, just what did you mean by 'none of your friends wanted to come'? Does that mean you don't consider us your friends?"

Anna considered rolling back an inch to two, just enough to be right on top of Connie's toes. Instead she looked at Brian to see his reaction to Connie's question. She was a little startled to see his cheeks aglow with a faint blush.

"Oh, gosh, no!" he responded. "I didn't mean that at all! I meant my guy friends!" His blush deepened, Connie laughed, and Anna felt more attracted to him than she ever had before.

She felt she needed to rescue him from Connie's clutches. "Just ignore her, Brian. She's just being acerbic."

Connie gave Anna a puzzled look and laughed again. "I'm being what?!"

"Never mind! Are you guys gonna sit with us or what?"

Rebecca finally found her voice and started to reply, "Yes, of course—"

"No, I think we'll sit in this pew behind you guys. We wouldn't want to crowd you two." She gave Anna a playful look and pulled Rebecca into their pew.

Anna considered arguing Connie's decision for a moment, then changed her mind. She loved her friends dearly, but a pew alone with Brian seemed much more appealing.

The first speaker stood up, and Brian laid his arm on the armrest between himself and Anna. As soon as she saw his tan arm resting so close to her own, Anna became entranced with it. She secretly studied every feature of his hand, wrist, and forearm. She imagined what she would do if he were to suddenly reach over and grab her own hand in his. At one point Brian turned his head and looked directly at her. She slowly looked back at him, and when their glances met, Brian rolled his eyes toward the ceiling. To say that his actions took Anna by surprise would be an understatement. Luckily for her, Brian quickly explained himself. He cocked a thumb over his shoulder and whispered, "Are your friends always this noisy?"

She had been so entranced with his arm, that she hadn't heard Connie and Rebecca at all. They were busily whispering and giggling, and probably had been since the fireside started. When she turned to look at them, Connie looked up at Anna, gave her a thumb's up, and went back to her giggling and whispering. Anna looked back at Brian, but she could only grin like an idiot and look down at her hands.

When the fireside was over, Brian bid them all farewell and went outside to meet his sister. Connie and Rebecca immediately pounced on Anna.

"So, Anna! Was this a planned meeting or a true coincidence as Brian would have us believe?"

"Connie, do me a favor. Would you please stick your left foot in front of my wheel? I got new tires today and I need to test them out."

Connie looked over at Rebecca with a look of triumph. "I told you, Becs! She planned the whole thing! A clandestine rendezvous with her true love!"

CHAPTER 6

Wednesday, May 17

Dear Diary,

The most incredible thing has happened! It all started three days ago at the regional fireside. Through a strange chain of events, I ended up sitting right next to Brian! It was fantastic! His regular group of friends decided not to show, and I just happened to be at the right place at the right time. I figured this would be my chance to get him to realize just how wonderful I really am. I was going to dazzle him right out of his socks. And you'll never guess how I did it! I sat like a big old, soggy bump on a log! I didn't say one word, let alone anything intelligent. I was so entranced by the very fact that he was sitting right next to me, that I don't even remember what the speakers said! But believe it or not, that is not the best part. Today was Sister Dailey's regular turn to help me exercise. You will never believe in a million years what she said to me! She said that when Brian got home from the fireside, he couldn't stop talking about how we sat together! He told her that Connie and Becca sat behind us, giggling and talking through the entire meeting. He was very impressed with how reverent and spiritual I had been. Apparently, clamming up was the best thing I could have done! Isn't that fabulous? Now let's see Connie tell me that Brian doesn't notice me. Not only is he aware of me, but it seems he has a favorable opinion! I could go on all day about Brian, but I'm sure you would like to read about something else for a change.

There is another dance coming up on Saturday night. I wonder what tactics Connie and Becca will try on me this time. Those two never give up. I guess that's why I love them so much. I just wish they would put their energy into something else besides trying to get me to go to a dance. Surely they must know that it would just be a waste of time.

School is going okay. Nothing to shout about.

Well, I hear the clank of dinner plates on the table, so I guess it's time to sign off.

The Church is true . . .
Anna

CHAPTER 7

ANNA, Connie, and Rebecca sat in front of the movie theater at Oakridge Mall, each busily gulping down an Orange Julius and handfuls of buttered popcorn.

"The super summer activity sounds like it's going to be a real blast," Becca started. "Hey, are you guys going to vote for the week at BYU or the week at Disneyland?"

"Definitely Disneyland!" Connie replied. "I've had a crush on Goofy for as long as I can remember."

"Don't you think you're setting your sights a little high, Con?" Rebecca asked tartly.

"Oh! Good one, Becs! Looks like I'm rubbing off on you after all!"

Rebecca just smiled sweetly.

"In case either of you is interested in my vote," Anna blurted out, "I think I have decided on BYU."

Connie looked at her in amazement. "You've got to be kidding! Why would you want to spend a week going to boring group activities when we could live it up in Southern California?"

Rebecca's chin dropped nearly to the floor. "Connie! How can you be so heartless? What is Anna going to be able to do at Disneyland when you are whooping it up with Goofy?"

Connie's eyes grew as big as saucers. "Oh, man, Anna. I am so sorry. I don't know what I was thinking about. Please forgive my stupid mouth!"

Anna smiled and patted Connie's arm. "Don't worry about it. It's no big deal. But that's not the only reason I've decided on BYU. I figure that, either way, my mom is going to have to come along to help me with certain things. And I just thought that it would be easier for us to be dorm-room buddies. Plus, anywhere we went in Southern California would be by car, which would mean my mother lifting me in and out of cars all day long."

Connie and Rebecca exchanged guilty looks. Connie cleared her throat. "Uh, I think I've changed my mind. BYU does sound like it would be fun. I'm going to vote for it."

"Me too," Rebecca added.

Anna looked from one to the other. Her two best friends were really trying to come through for her. "You guys don't have to do that. Whichever way it turns out will be fine. Really."

"Nope. I've decided," Connie stated defiantly. "I'm going to vote for BYU, and don't try to change my mind."

"You guys are the best friends a girl could hope for."

All three girls sat grinning at each other. Finally Connie broke the silence.

"All right, already! That's enough sap for one afternoon. So, Anna, do you plan on trapping Brian in a lip lock under the bleachers at the Cougar football field?" Connie threw her head back and laughed. She straightened up and glanced over at Anna just in time to see the piece of popcorn as it flew through the air towards her face.

GARY HARMON arrived at the mall just as the three girls were coming out. As he lifted Anna into the car, she continued to talk a mile a minute with Connie and Rebecca.

"What exactly are you girls chattering away about, anyway?"

"First of all, Dad, we are not girls. We are young women."

Gary chuckled. "Well, excuse me, young ladies."

"That's okay. And we're talking about this year's super summer activity. We've all decided to vote for the week at BYU."

Gary looked over at his daughter in amazement. "Really? BYU? What was the other choice?"

"Disneyland!" Connie yelled from the backseat. "But all three of us decided that it would be rough for Sister Harmon to be lifting Anna in and out of the car all day long. So BYU would be a more logical choice. Plus there's the obvious fact that Anna wouldn't be able to go on most of the rides. How much fun would she have just watching everyone else?"

At this point the three girls broke off into their own conversation about the upcoming activity. Had any of them ever glanced at Gary Harmon, they would have been shocked; he was gripping the steering wheel so tightly that his knuckles had turned white. His jaw was solidly clenched shut, a bright blue vein was throbbing in his right temple, and tiny beads of sweat were popping out on his top lip. Connie's words had been like a dagger through his heart. He kept hearing her voice over and over in his mind.

. . . BYU would be a more logical choice . . .
. . . the obvious fact . . .
. . . couldn't go on the rides . . .
. . . how much fun would she have . . .
. . . how much fun . . .
. . . how much fun?

It's all my fault that she can't have fun, he thought. It's all my fault she can't go to Disneyland. It's all my fault her mother has to lift her in and out of cars. It's all my fault . . . it's all my fault . . . it's all my fault!

CHAPTER 8

WHEN Gary saw his wife's car pull into the driveway, he rushed to finish getting everything set in the living room.

Emily pushed Anna into the house, and Gary pounced on them almost immediately. "How was school today, princess?"

"Dad? What are you doing home? Are you sick?"

"No, no. I just came home a little early today, that's all."

Emily took Anna's school books and purse and put them on the hallway table.

"Don't let him fool you, dear. Your father came home early because he has a surprise for you in the living room, and he wanted to be here to see your expression."

Anna's face brightened up the word "surprise." Just like any teenager, the mention of a present was enough to brighten her day.

"Can I have it now?" Anna was chomping at the bit. If her dad wanted to see her expression, it had to be something spectacular. That ruled out clothes, for sure. Maybe it was a diamond pendant! Or maybe that new sewing machine that had ten million features on it.

"Close your eyes and I'll push you in there. Emily, walk in front of us and make sure she keeps her eyes closed." Both women did as they were instructed, and after a few moments Anna's chair came to rest in the center of the living room.

"Okay, Anna, open your eyes."

She slowly opened them to find she was face to face with a shiny, new exercise bike. It was sitting on top of the coffee table. She was completely amazed, letting out a squeal of delight. "Oh, Dad! It's fabulous! This is for me?"

"Yeah. I figured you could use it to keep up your upper body strength. That's why it's up on the table. You can set the tension to where you want it, then push the pedals around with your hands."

"Why, Gary! What a wonderful idea!"

Anna held her arms open and Gary rushed over to hug her. "Are you happy, Anna? Do you really like it?"

She kissed him softly on the cheek. "I love it, Daddy. Thank you so much."

"You are welcome."

Emily grabbed Gary by the sleeve and pulled him towards the hallway. "Where are you taking me?"

"I'm glad you're home early. I washed all the bedroom curtains this morning, and I need you to help me hang them back up. Let's leave Anna to play with her new toy."

"Let me know if you need help, Anna!" Gary yelled as he was dragged down the hallway.

Anna played with buttons, levers, and knobs. As she tested the tension and the padding that her father had put on the pedals, Jason came bursting in the door, tossing his bookbag on the hall table next to Anna's. He poked his head into the living room.

"Hi, Anna. Where's Mom . . . Hey! Cool! What's that for?" He trooped over to the bike and started fidgeting with the levers.

"Hands off, runt. Dad bought it to help maintain my upper body strength."

Jason eyed her suspiciously. "When did you ask him for this thing?"

Anna reached over and slapped his hand away from the timer. "I didn't ask him for it. He just surprised me with it today."

This little bit of news was obviously not what Jason wanted to hear. He flew into a terrible rage. "I knew it!" he screamed. "This is so unfair, Anna!"

His reaction to the situation surprised Anna. "Jason, calm down! What is your problem?"

Now Jason was stomping back and forth between the bike and the couch. "My problem? I'll tell you my problem! Dad is totally unfair! He treats you like a little princess, and he practically ignores me! That's my problem!"

"Oh, stop acting like such a little brat. You're just jealous because Dad bought me something and not you."

He stopped pacing and looked her square in the face. "You're right, Anna. That's exactly it. Did you know that just yesterday I asked Dad for one of those pitching nets for the backyard? He told me flat out 'No!' because we couldn't afford it. And now he brings you this. You know what, sometimes I wish that I had gotten hurt in that accident, too. Then Dad would buy me presents!"

Anna stared at her brother, completely stunned. "You don't mean that," she whispered. "You're being ridiculous, Jason."

"Am I?" he snapped. "Think about it, Anna. When the youth went on a white water rafting trip, and you cried because you were in that chair and couldn't go, you suddenly got your computer. Four months ago when the youth spent the weekend in Monterey at a dance workshop, you suddenly got the television for your bedroom. The list goes on and on! And now all of a sudden you get this bike. I don't know what happened this time, but it must have been pretty big for Dad to buy you this!"

One tear slowly rolled down her cheek. "You don't know what you're talking about, Jason. Dad's not like that, and you know it."

"He is, Anna! Can't you see . . ."

Suddenly Emily appeared from around the corner. "Hey! What's all the yelling about?"

Jason looked at his mother, then dashed for the front door. He jumped on his bike and pedaled down the street.

"What was his problem?"

Anna motioned for her mom to sit down on the couch. She rolled her chair right next to her mother so that they could talk without being overheard.

"Mom, why did Dad buy this bike for me?"

Emily gave her daughter a bewildered look. "Anna, your father told you why he bought it. To help you exercise . . ."

"Mom, please. If we couldn't afford a pitching net for Jason, why did I get this bike? And what about the computer, and the television?"

"Anna, what are you getting at?"

Anna sat quietly for a few seconds, trying to muster up the nerve to ask the next question. She also wondered if her mom would tell her the truth. She sighed heavily and closed her eyes. "Is Dad buying me these things because he feels guilty about the accident?" She opened her eyes to see a shocked expression on her mother's face.

"Anna Kendal Harmon! I can't believe you asked me that!"

"Mom, I just need to know. Jason believes that he is. He brought up some good points that I never thought about before. Please, Mom. Please tell me the truth."

Emily opened her mouth to protest again, but the lump that had risen in her throat prevented her from speaking. Her chin began to tremble uncontrollably. "Anna, please. Let me explain . . ."

Anna held up her hand to stop her mother from speaking. "That's all the answer I need." Now her own chin began to tremble as she turned her chair and headed for the front door.

"Anna, please don't go. Let's talk about this."

"I just need some time alone to think. I'll be back later."

She wheeled her chair down the front walk and onto the sidewalk. Her tears were flowing freely now, and as she headed down the sidewalk she contemplated where she should go. Most everything was too far away for her to push herself. She decided on the elementary school four streets over. At this time of day the playground would be deserted.

By the time she realized that she was on Brian's street, it was too late to turn back. She saw his house, which was now about three houses down from where she was. A few guys were on the lawn playing football, but they were all roughly the same size, so it was impossible to tell if one of them was Brian. One of the guys spotted her and waved. She quickly panned the street to see if he could have possibly been waving at someone else. The street was unmercifully empty, so she shyly waved back.

I have no idea who that is, but please don't let it be Brian! she thought. She slowly rolled forward, since it was too late to turn back. When she got close enough to distinguish faces, she realized that the boy who had waved was

Brian's best friend, Karl. The other boys she recognized from school, but she didn't know their names. When she reached the house, Karl crossed the lawn and met her at the sidewalk.

"Hi, Anna. Where are you going?"

She put on her friendliest smile, then lied through her teeth. "I'm just out on a little stroll around the neighborhood. It's such a nice day and I couldn't stand to be in the house."

"Yeah. I know what you mean."

The screen door on the house slammed, and Anna looked past Karl to see Brian coming down the lawn, carrying four cans of soda. Just the sight of him made her catch her breath in her throat. As soon as Brian spied her, he headed immediately in her direction.

"Anna! What are you doing here?"

She nervously tapped the arm of her chair. "Just out for a stroll."

"Hey, Brian! How about those sodas?" one of the boys on the lawn yelled.

"Yeah, yeah. Just hold your noise! Karl, would you mind taking these drinks up there?"

After Karl was gone, Brian gazed into Anna's eyes. "Now, why don't you tell me why you're really out here?"

Anna was amazed at how well he had seen through her facade. But for some reason she felt compelled to convince him otherwise. "Really, Brian. I was just out for a walk around the block."

"Anna, please. You have obviously been crying."

Anna's hand went immediately to her face. She held out for about two seconds before her chin began to tremble and one tiny tear rolled slowly down her hot cheek. He stood up and grabbed the handgrips of her chair.

"Let's go for a walk, okay?"

Anna could only nod, her eyes fixed on her lap.

"Hey, you guys! I'm gonna go for a walk with this young lady! Feel free to stay as long as you want!"

"No sweat, Brian!" Karl yelled. The others just waved him off.

"Where would you like to go?" Brian was pushing her in the direction of the school, so she told him that the elementary playground would be fine.

"Okay, but when we get there, I want you to tell me what upset you."

The whole way to the playground, Anna wondered whether or not she should actually tell him the entire story. After all, her family had kept the exact details of the accident a secret until now. She knew in her heart how her father felt, and she knew that he wouldn't want her to tell the story to anyone. But on the other hand, she had kept it bottled up inside over the past couple of years. It would be a relief to finally talk about it.

The playground was oddly full of kids, so they headed instead to the baseball field. By the time they reached the perfect shady spot on the grass, she had reached her decision.

CHAPTER 9

I'M NOT really sure how to begin. But the important thing to keep in mind is this: all the stories you've heard so far about the reason I'm in this wheelchair are false. You may have even heard some directly from my family. That was all my father's idea. He told us all what we could and couldn't say about the accident."

"Gosh, Anna. This is unbelievable! You mean to tell me that this is some deep, dark secret that your family has been hiding this whole time?"

Anna had to put her hand over her mouth to hide the giggle that threatened to come out. He was listening so intently, and the expression on his face was the same as someone who was completely engrossed in a murder mystery.

"Well, it's not as exciting and melodramatic as that, but my father doesn't want it spread around."

"If that is a hint to keep a lid on what I am about to hear, you have my word of honor."

She could see by the look in his eye that he was serious. And she had never once heard him gossip or even say an unkind word about anyone.

She sighed deeply, contemplated her first words, then began to unwind the events of that tragic night.

"As everyone knows, the accident happened about three-and-a-half years ago. We had gone to Utah for my dad's family reunion. It was incredibly hot that time of year, so my dad spent practically the entire week in a lake by our campsite. He even went night swimming a couple of times. My mom tried to stop him. In fact, she teased him that if he got sick, she would spank him like a child. And sure enough, on the last day of the reunion, my father woke up with a head cold. His sinuses were totally congested, and he said his head pounded with every beat of his heart. Both my dad and my older brother, Troy, had to work the following day, and as it was we were going to have to drive all night to get home on time. So we couldn't wait in Utah while my dad got better. My Uncle Chester gave my dad a couple of cold pills that were advertised as the non-drowsy kind. My mom was worried, of course, and objected to him taking them, even as he swallowed the last one. She told him that if he felt the slightest bit drowsy, he was to pull over immediately and let either her or Troy drive. Even though my dad agreed to her conditions, I knew he would never give up the driver's seat. My dad comes from the 'old school' where the man of the house is expected to do things like drive the entire distance of a family trip, even if that means driving for 14 hours straight."

Brian nodded in agreement. "I know what you mean. My dad is exactly the same way."

"He was fine for the first couple of hours. In fact, he actually started to feel pretty good. The pills were really working on his nose, and his headache was just a faint tapping behind his right eye. But it seemed like as soon as the sun sank, so did my dad. Everyone else had fallen asleep, myself included. But for some strange reason, I was jolted awake. At first I thought we had hit something, but no one else had woken up. I adjusted my pillow and started to lay back down, when I happened to catch my dad's reflection in the rearview mirror. His eyes were half-open. And let me tell you, he was struggling to keep them open that far. I knew that the ice chest in the back seat still had some sodas left in it, and I figured that drinking one might perk him up a little. So I unlatched my seatbelt, turned around, and started to reach for the cooler. From that point on I can only remember bits and pieces. I remember hitting the cement divider, then being thrown as the car bounced back onto the freeway. I can also remember the tremendous crashing noises of the other cars hitting us. But I guess I have blocked out the rest. I assume that at the exact moment I was reaching for the soda, my dad fell completely asleep. The next thing I knew, I woke up in a hospital bed with tubes and needles sticking out all over me.

"Both my parents were sitting next to my bed, and when I looked up at them they started to cry. A few hours later I learned that my lower spine had been broken in two places. At first the doctors gave me a fifty-fifty chance of ever walking again. But as time went on and feeling didn't return to my legs, they changed their story. It's pretty definite that I'll never walk again.

"But getting back to the hospital, it seems that I had been completely out for almost three days. Boy, talk about disorientation! It was really weird! Three days were just gone! My oldest brother, Troy, tried to make me feel better by telling me that I didn't miss much—just Jason playing video games and throwing his usual temper tantrums, Mom's burnt meatloaf, and Dad's lectures on the importance of good oral hygiene. Of course I knew he was lying. From the haggard looks on their faces, it was obvious they had spent all of their waking hours right by my side.

"We thought the worst was over, but for me, the worst was just about to begin. I endured hours and hours of painful therapy—all the stretching, and exercising, and pulling, and pushing. It was an absolute nightmare."

As Anna described her therapy ordeal, Brian's face grimaced and frowned as if he were experiencing the pain.

"All total, I believe I spent about eight and a half months in the hospital. Happily for me, therapy was reduced to three hard-core sessions a week. It has slowly reduced over the years to twice a week, then once a week, and now finally just exercises on my own. I still go in for check-ups about once every month or two."

Brian was completely flabbergasted. "Wow, Anna. What a trial that must have been for you! That's enough to make anyone cry. Is that what happened today? All of the old, painful memories came flooding back?"

"No, not quite. It has to do with my father. He feels so guilty for putting me in this chair; I'm sure he believes he has ruined not only my childhood, but the rest of my life as well. I've noticed before that he doesn't like to hear anyone talk about my wheelchair, even in passing. I used to think that it was because he was embarrassed of me. But I know different now. He must feel responsible for ending any chance of life for me at age twelve."

"So is that what made you cry today?" Brian asked hesitantly.

"No, that's not it either. The reason I was crying today was because I just found out that ever since the accident, my father has ignored my little brother, Jason. It seems that my dad has been buying me big, expensive gifts every time he heard of an upcoming activity that I wouldn't be able to do. I never associated the two, and that's pure stupidity on my part. But apparently Jason noticed. He even went as far as to tell me that he wished he had been hurt in the accident as well. That way my dad would pay attention to him."

Brian's flabbergasted look turned to one of utter horror. "You've got to be kidding! He said that?"

"Yep. Just this afternoon. Until then I never realized how he really felt. I don't think anyone did."

"That poor little kid. Can you imagine wanting attention from your own father so badly, that you would actually wish yourself in a wheelchair?"

"I know he didn't really mean it. But I still feel responsible somehow. I must have been a real bonehead not to make the connection with all those gifts."

Brian had been plucking pieces of grass and tearing them into little pieces. He stopped now and looked up at her, shook his head and clucked his tongue, then went back to picking grass. "How can you say that, Anna? How can you blame yourself? It sounds to me like your father needs to take the blame, and I'm not saying this to be rude. Your dad has a lot of unresolved feelings all penned up inside, and they're affecting his decision-making ability."

"So are you saying my dad needs a therapist?" Anna asked rather sarcastically.

"Please, Anna, don't be angry with me. I certainly don't mean to insult you or your father. But think about it realistically. You said that your father won't talk about the accident or your wheelchair. He made the whole family keep up the charade because of his overwhelming guilt. Anna, that's not normal."

Anna dropped her gaze from him. She knew he was right, and she regretted her sarcastic tone. In fact, on several occasions she had thought it would be good for her father to see a therapist. She knew it wasn't right for her father to lie about the accident. But how do you tell your dad that he is being unreasonable and needs to see a psychiatrist?

"I'm sorry, Brian. I'm not mad at you. In fact, I agree with you totally. I guess it's just hard to hear someone else say that your dad is a crackpot." She laughed a little at this, even though it wasn't really funny. Maybe she was simply trying to ease a serious conversation. Maybe because she was just as crazy. Or maybe it was some of the old nervousness coming back that stemmed from being so close to Brian. Whatever it was, Brian responded and smiled back.

"Your dad is not a crackpot. He just needs someone to talk to, that's all."

"Have you ever thought about being a therapist, Brian? You sure made me feel better."

Brian's smile widened. "In that case, that will be one hundred dollars, please."

Anna raised her eyebrows and laughed. "No, really. You're good at saying what people need to hear. Maybe you could even be one of those guys who talks to terrorists holding hostages. Or even the guy who talks jumpers down off of ledges."

Brian laughed as he got to his feet. "Well, have you ever thought about being an employment specialist? You seem to have the knack of finding the right job for the right person."

He unlocked her back wheels, grabbed the handgrips, and pushed on her chair. But it didn't budge. Apparently the ground had been just soft enough for the two rear wheels to sink in about an inch.

"Uh-oh. You're stuck, Anna. What should I do?"

Anna looked over the left side of her chair and saw the wheel. "Oh, man. I don't know. I've never been stuck in mud before. I guess just give me a good, hard shove."

"Okay! You got it!" He backed up three steps, kicked up his feet like a bull about to charge, then ran at the back of the chair. It was a great idea, and it probably would have worked if Brian had hit the chair a little lower. But he hit it about three quarters of the way up on the back support. The wheelchair stayed right where it was, but Anna was thrown out of her seat. She let out a shrill scream and threw her arms out straight to catch herself, but still managed to land on her stomach with a thump.

"Anna!" Brian called, and ran around to where she was laying on the ground. "Oh, my gosh! I am so, so sorry!" he kept repeating as he helped her turn over to a sitting position.

"I'm okay, Brian. Just a little embarrassed."

"But you have no reason to be embarrassed! I'm the one who knocked you down. I'm the one who's embarrassed! I am so sorry."

She looked back at the wheelchair, still stuck in the dirt. It stared back at her, almost laughing.

"What do we do now?" he asked her lamely.

Anna looked from Brian to the wheelchair, then back to Brian. "I . . . need you to lift me back into the chair."

Brian's eyes grew wide and then he looked at the chair. "But what if I drop you?"

Anna smiled, trying to reassure him. "You won't drop me. I'll hook my arms around your neck. Besides, I'm not that heavy!"

Brian smiled and seemed to relax a little. "Okay. Tell me what to do first."

"First, get the chair out of the mud."

Brian jumped up and set the chair on firmer ground. "Done. Now what?"

"Just pick me up. Put one arm around my back and the other under my knees. And please don't worry about dropping me."

Brian squatted down beside her and positioned his arms as he was instructed. Anna slid her arms around his neck. This was the closest she had ever been to him. Her heart began to beat wildly in her chest. She was tempted to pucker up and plant a kiss right on his bronze cheek, and she blushed at the thought.

"Hold on, Anna! Here we go!" With a small grunt, Brian picked her up and headed for the chair. "You're right! You are pretty light. I could carry you all day!"

Anna giggled nervously. "Just to the chair would be fine, thanks."

He bent over the side of the chair and set her down softly. "Are you sure you're okay? I'm really sorry."

Anna smiled and looked down at her lap. "I'm fine. But I think I'd like to go home now."

"Sure. I'll walk you, if that's okay."

ASIDE FROM AN OCCASIONAL word or two, the walk home was a silent one. Anna was extremely grateful that it was only four blocks. When they finally reached her house, Anna awkwardly thanked him for listening to her story and walking her home.

"You're welcome. And there's no need to thank me for dumping you over."

Anna looked up to see him grinning, and she had to crack a smile.

"I'm going home now. You probably have a lot to talk about with your parents."

Anna nodded in agreement.

"But I'll see you tomorrow at school."

"I'll be there. See you later, Brian. And thanks again."

CHAPTER 10

Wednesday, May 24

Dear Diary,

Remember yesterday when I wrote about spending the afternoon at the school with Brian and telling him what happened to me? And then he dumped me on the ground? Well, the story continues. When I got home from the walk, my parents were waiting for me in the living room. I don't know why, but for some reason I thought I was dead meat. But we actually sat down together and talked everything over. My father has been denying it all for so long, that his first instinct was to ignore that any problem existed. But my mom and I eventually were able to break through. I'm not saying that we solved everything; that would be impossible in one afternoon. However, we at least talked about our feelings. And believe it or not, I even asked my dad if he would consider going to group counseling. I thought for sure that he would refuse. My dad is not exactly the open-minded type. But he actually said that he would think about it! I know that's not as good as a commitment, but it's a lot more than I ever expected. We have a long way to go, but at least we have finally started.

There is even more good news, though! This morning my mom went out to warm up the car so she could take me to school. When she came back, she was carrying three red roses and a little note. She said she found them on the front porch. I was so shocked when she handed them to me! When I print up this page I'll attach the note, but this is what it said:

Dear Anna,

I am so sorry for what happened yesterday.
Please forgive me—

Brian

My mouth went dry and my palms started to perspire! Isn't he the sweetest guy? But wait! It gets better! After fourth period today, I went to my locker to get my lunch. Brian met me there and asked if we could have lunch together! If I could have, I would have done cartwheels down the hallway! Unfortunately, we weren't alone. Connie, Rebecca, Karl Tanner, and some guy named Garrett were there also. Karl is in our ward, but Garrett is just Brian's school friend. Brian sat right next to me, though. And I'll tell you something else, unless I'm totally losing it, I could have sworn that Karl and Rebecca were making eyes at each other when they thought no one else was looking. Wouldn't it be cool if we all went out on a double date sometime? It could happen! And then naturally we would have a double wedding! But not until we were all through with school, of course. I'll have to tell Becca that I saw her flirting so that she can help me plan all of this. Okay, I know I'm getting mental now, so I'll move on.

After lunch, Brian and I have art class together, so he walked me there! But the juiciest part came after class. As I said before, I don't like to enter or leave a classroom at the same time the other students do, so after class I always wait around until everyone leaves. Well, today Brian took his time putting his stuff away, so we were among the last students there. He came over to my table and asked what I would be doing after school. I said that after my exercises, nothing. He said that he really enjoyed talking to me yesterday, and that he wanted us to become better friends. Then he asked if he could come over today! He also said that he felt bad that we had been in the same ward for so long, and yet we hardly know each other. Can you believe it? I was shocked! Needless to say, I could hardly wait for my exercises to be over. Brian finally showed up around 4:30. I won't go into detail about every second, there are some things that a woman prefers to keep private. (Plus, I was being such a spaz that I can't remember everything!) But a few major points: my mom made us a great snack, we played video games with Jason, and we talked a lot about the super summer activity. Brian is going to vote for Disneyland, of course. I was pleasantly surprised that when I told him I was going to vote for BYU, he didn't even ask why! He just said that either one would be fun, and he's really looking forward to it. Brian is such a great guy. You would expect a sixteen-year-old boy to be obnoxious and maybe even rebellious. But Brian is the most sensitive and genuinely caring person. And he is also very spiritual. He is the guy who gets up every Fast Sunday to bear his testimony and tears up at everyone else's. He is every LDS mother's dream child. (Not to mention every LDS girl's dream husband.) But you know what, even if nothing romantic ever comes of this, I am really glad that Brian wants to be my friend.

Oh, man! I just remembered something else that happened! My mom was talking to Brian while we were eating, and she offered to pick him up and drive him to school! Aaahhh! I almost died! Having him in the car that would not be bad, but having him see my mom lifting me in and out of my chair will be embarrassing. We'll see how it goes. Tomorrow will be the first day we pick him up. I'll be sure to write how it goes.

The Church is true . . .
Anna

CHAPTER 11

"You know, Sister Harmon, you've been picking me up for almost two weeks now."

Emily turned left on Meridian Avenue and headed towards the high school. "Yes, I know, Brian. And it's been a pleasure."

"Well, thanks! But that's not why I brought it up. I've been thinking that since I have to get out of the car anyway . . ."

Anna felt her stomach turn over. "Uh, what exactly are you driving at, Brian?" she interrupted, knowing full well what his answer would be.

"I was wondering if you two would object to me putting Anna in her chair when we get to school," he replied bluntly, as if it were the most normal request in the world.

Mother and daughter looked at each other to see the other's reaction.

"Oh, I don't know, Brian," Emily responded. "That makes me very nervous."

Thank you Mother! Thank you! Anna thought and sighed with relief. Unfortunately for her, Brian was not easily discouraged.

"Well, you know, Sister Harmon, it's not as if I've never done it before. I'm sure she told you about that day at the elementary school."

Emily smiled at Brian in the rearview mirror. "Yes, she did. And she also said that you were the reason that she ate grass in the first place."

Brian grinned widely and blushed. "It was an accident! Besides, that doesn't have anything to do with how well I put her back in the chair!"

"You are right about that," Emily conceded. "Anna described you as 'strong yet graceful.'"

Anna's eyes bulged out of her head. "Mom!"

"Oh. Was I not supposed to say that?" she asked coyly.

"Well, then that should convince you!" Brian interjected.

Anna shot her mom a look that said, Don't you dare agree to this! Emily could only shrug her shoulders.

"Well, I guess it would be okay. But Brian, you have to promise to be very careful."

"I do! I do!"

Anna slumped down in her seat and folded her arms over her chest with a hhmpff! Emily just looked over at her daughter and shrugged again. She mouthed the word "sorry." Anna rolled her eyes and turned her head to look out the window.

This is going to be the worst day of my life! It's bad enough to have him watch every time my mom puts me in that dumb chair, but now he wants to do it himself! And my own mother practically threw me in his lap!

As soon as they pulled up in front of the school, Brian jumped out of the car. He ran around the rear, opened the tailgate, and pulled out her chair.

"I had better help him with your chair. We wouldn't want it collapsing on you."

Anna offered her mother a sarcastic sneer. "This conversation is not over, Mom."

"I didn't think it would be"

Emily stood by nervously as Brian hooked one arm under Anna's legs, and the other arm around her back. Anna put her right arm around his neck and braced herself for anything. Brian took a deep breath, held it, and lifted. Anna felt herself lift about an inch off the seat before she was viciously snapped back. As he backed up to see what had gone wrong, Brian hit his head on the door frame. Anna's look of bewilderment turned to heated embarrassment when she followed Brian's gaze to the seatbelt which was still securely fastened over her shoulder and stomach.

"Shall we try it again? This time without the seatbelt?"

Emily peered over his shoulder. "Seatbelt? You forgot to take off your seatbelt?!" She started to laugh hysterically.

"You are being an incredible help today, Mom." She took off the seatbelt and looked at Brian. "I'm ready now."

Brian eyed her, then the rest of the front seat. "Are you sure?"

"Yes!"

He repeated all of his previous steps, right up to holding his breath. He lifted her out of the seat, stood up straight, and turned around to face Emily.

"See? I told you I could do it!"

"Okay, now just ease her into the chair before anything else happens."

He did as he was told, making sure to set her down in the center of the chair.

"Taa daa!" he exclaimed triumphantly, throwing his arms into the air.

"Well done, Brian," Emily responded.

"All right!" He clapped his hands together. "Looks like I have a permanent job!" he yelled as he ducked his head into the back seat to get his books.

Anna and her mother looked at each other at the same time, each reflecting the other's horrified expression.

CHAPTER 12

"As soon as you write down your choice, immediately fold it in half and raise your hand. I'll come around and collect them. And remember, this is an individual vote. No pressuring allowed."

Connie and Anna exchanged amused glances. From somewhere in the back of the room, a faceless voice started to chant "Disneyland!" Then one by one everyone started to join in. "Disneyland! Disneyland! Disneyland!"

"That's enough! That's quite enough!" Sister Campbell had to yell over the crowd. "Please just write down your vote and raise your hand."

Anna looked down at her ballot. She slowly wrote down "BYU." She stared at it for a couple of seconds, then looked over at Brian and Karl. Both had already finished voting, and they were busily whispering to each other about the Disneyland trip. Brian happened to catch Anna's glance and gave her a little wave. She waved back and looked down at her ballot. She tapped her pen on the desk, trying to talk herself out of what she was about to do.

I guess it could be fun. There are lots of shows I could see. Lots of . . . lots of . . . lots of shows I could see. She looked again from Connie and Rebecca to Brian.

"Do I have all of the ballots?" Sister Campbell asked from the front of the room.

Anna scribbled out "BYU" and quickly wrote down "Disneyland," then raised her hand.

Connie and Rebecca walked out of the classroom ahead of Anna, then hurried down the hallway towards the chapel.

"Connie! Becs! Wait up, you guys!"

Both girls looked back at Anna with guilty expressions. "You tell her."

"I'm not gonna tell her. You tell her."

"But it was your idea! You tell her!"

Anna finally caught up with them while they were still arguing. "What are you two talking about? Tell me what?"

Rebecca took a small step backward and nudged Connie in the back. "Well, you see, Anna . . . we sort of . . . uh . . . voted for Disneyland."

"Please don't be mad at us!" Rebecca added immediately.

Anna looked at them and couldn't help but laugh.

"What's so funny?" Connie asked coolly.

"You guys! I voted for Disneyland, too!"

Rebecca clasped her hands together. "You did? But I thought you were set on BYU. What made you change your mind?"

"You know what? I'm really not sure. I guess there were just so many people that wanted Disneyland, I didn't want to be the spoilsport."

Connie looked at Anna in amazement. "You are so cool, girl!"

Rebecca bent over and gave her a quick hug. "Anna, we will have so much fun, even if you can't go on all the rides. Plus, Disneyland is just one activity they have planned for the whole week. I'm sure you won't have any trouble doing the rest of the junk."

"Yeah!" Connie added enthusiastically. "We're supposed to go to Muscle Beach and the Movieland Wax Museum, and I think there is supposed to be a party with the youth down there."

Anna started towards the chapel again. "You two don't have to try to talk me into it. I know it will be fun. Besides, we don't even know which activity won yet. So let's go into sacrament meeting and hear the results."

NATURALLY, THE DISNEYLAND trip won by a landslide. The final vote was sixty-three to nine. Immediately after Bishop Caldwell made the announcement, kids throughout the chapel turned to each other and began whispering. Anna wrote a note to her mother on the back of the ward bulletin and passed it to her.

"I hope you're not disappointed, Mom. I know you were looking forward to seeing Grandma in Utah. Are you still going with me?"

Emily's reply came back: "Of course I'm going! I love Disneyland!"

After church Anna was practically attacked by Connie and Rebecca.

"Let's go out by your car and plan our wardrobe!" Rebecca pushed Anna's chair at warp speed. Connie had to jog to keep up.

"Slow down, Becs, old girl! We don't leave for another month or so! Heck! We have to get through school first!"

"I know that! But a woman's wardrobe is an important part of finding her mate! Besides, we only have another week and a half of school."

"Hi, girls."

All three whipped around to see Brian and Karl approaching. Connie nudged Anna from the left and Rebecca nudged her from the right.

"Ouch, you knuckleheads!" she whispered hoarsely.

"Anna, I just wanted to make sure you were okay with the decision that was made. I know you were counting on BYU."

"Actually Brian, Anna voted for Disneyland," Rebecca jumped in. Even though she had addressed Brian, her gaze never left Karl.

"You did? What made you change your mind? That day at your house you sounded so dead set on BYU."

"I'll give you one guess," Connie replied.

"Well," Anna exclaimed while throwing Connie the evil eye, "I just thought it over and decided that a majority of us would want Disneyland. Plus, it's not as if I ever thought the whole trip would be a drag. Just the parts that involve the Matterhorn and Space Mountain."

"Well, that's great! I'm glad you're not upset and I'm glad you're still going. Hey! Why don't we all travel down in the same van? It would be a blast!"

"Okay!" Karl and Rebecca responded together, then looked at each other and blushed.

"But you know, Brian, my mom has to travel with me. Would you guys mind if she rode in the same car?"

"Not at all! Your mom's cool. Well, my dad is waiting for me, so I guess I'll see you tomorrow at school."

"Bye, Rebecca."

"Bye, Karl."

After they were gone Connie pulled a lovesick face. "Bye, Rebecca! Bye, Karl! Kiss, kiss! And you, Miss 'Would you mind if my mom came?' What did you expect him to say?"

"Careful Con, your claws are showing," Anna retorted.

"We really need to find you a man, Connie."

"Oh, let me guess, Becs. I need to update my wardrobe."

"You really hate it when I'm right, don't you?"

"I sure do, and luckily for me it's not that often."

"Okay, you dorks, knock it off. I thought we came out here to talk about the trip."

"I thought we were going to talk about Becca's wardrobe!"

From a few cars away Rebecca's mother shouted, "Rebecca! Let's go! Your father is starving!"

"Looks like you two will have to talk about my wardrobe without me. Be sure to let me know what you plan for me to wear to Disneyland!" And with a wave she was gone.

"Okay, Anna, she's gone. Spill the beans."

"Connie, what the heck are you talking about?"

Connie bounced impatiently from one foot to the other. "You know, Rebecca and Karl! She nearly flips her wig every time he comes around! And now that you and Brian are so chummy, I was wondering if he ever said anything."

"No, he never has. But wouldn't it be great if they hit it off?" Anna thought back to her plans for a double wedding. "Connie, have you ever thought about where you would want to go for your honeymoon?"

Connie threw back her head and laughed. "Where in the world did that come from?"

Anna grinned. "I was just wondering where I should tell Brian to take me!"

"You are a sly, conniving old fox, my dear!"

"Hey, I've learned from the best, Connie!"

Connie was silent for a moment before responding, "A cruise."

"What?"

"Make Brian take you on a cruise!"

CHAPTER 13

"JASON! Turn off that video game! You know we're waiting for you!"

"But, Mom!"

"No buts! Let's go!"

Jason flipped off the game and television and sulked all the way to the front hallway. "Why are we having family home evening so early, anyway?" he whined.

Emily handed him his jacket. "I told you, your father made a special appointment for us all and we have to be there by five o'clock."

Anna was busily searching through her purse. She finally found her bounty and pulled out a well used tube of lip balm. "Where is Dad, Mom?"

"He will leave straight from work and meet us there. Get your shoes on please, Jason."

Jason scowled down the hall to his bedroom.

"What's all the secrecy about, Mom?"

"Well, your father planned this a few weeks ago. It was hard for him to finally go through with it, and he desperately wants it all to work out."

Anna gave her mother a completely puzzled look. "You should have been a politician, Mom. You just said a whole bunch of nothing, and you didn't tell me one thing about tonight."

Emily laughed as she got her sweater out of the closet. "Your dad wants tonight to be a surprise, and he would kill me if I spoiled it. Jason! Get the lead out, young man!"

Anna and Jason continued to needle their mother for the entire car ride, even as they pulled up in front of the gray office building. Jason slumped down in his seat when they found a parking spot.

"Oh, great. A group dentist appointment."

They met Gary in the building's lobby. All four Harmons loaded into the elevator and rode it to the second floor. Gary led them to an office on the far left of the hallway. The nameplate on the door read "Adam Brooks, Ph.D."

"Ph.D.?" Jason looked up at his dad. "I thought the little letters for a dentist were D.D.S."

Gary and Emily exchanged amused glances. "You told the kids we were going to the dentist?"

"No, not really. Jason just assumed that's where we were going, and I never corrected him."

"Oh, gosh!" Anna exclaimed. "Isn't 'Ph.D.' for some sort of therapist?"

Gary turned so that he was facing his family head on. "Yes, Anna. That's right."

"But I'm not nutso!" Jason cried defiantly. "Why do I have to see a shrink?"

Gary put his hands on his son's shoulders. "Jason, no one here is nutso. It's just that your mother and I have decided that we all need someone to talk to—someone outside the family."

A smile began to spread slowly across Anna's face. "Dad, are we really going to talk to a therapist?"

Gary smiled back at his daughter and stroked her hair. "Yes, Princess, we really are. But we had better get in there or else we'll miss our appointment." He opened the door and allowed his family to pass before walking in.

"Now," Dr. Brooks explained, "for our first meeting I want to spend the time getting to know you all. But I do want you to feel as if you got your money's worth. So, each one of you, starting with the children, will recount to me exactly what you remember about the accident. Start with the morning it happened and end whenever you feel it appropriate. There will be no analyzing and no diagnosis made today, so just relax and be yourself. Take as long as you like and try to be as accurate as you possibly can be. The only thing I ask of each of you is to remain silent while someone else is talking.

With four different people involved, there are bound to be discrepancies. Just wait until your turn, then you can say as much as you want."

One by one the Harmons began to unravel the events leading up to and including the accident. And sure enough, just as Dr. Brooks had warned, there were differences in every story. Each one described exactly what they felt and saw during the whole ordeal. Interestingly enough, even though there were four relatively different stories, there were only two endings. Both Emily and Jason chose to end their account on the day Jason had accused Gary of giving Anna "guilt gifts." Gary and Anna both talked of the events leading right up to walking in the office that very day. But regardless of even the smallest differences or similarities, one thing remained constant in all cases: at one point or another in their story, the storyteller always started to cry. Naturally the tears came at the point of the story that the storyteller found the most painful for them to remember. With Jason that point came when he started to talk about being ignored by his father and feeling like his father stopped loving him after the accident. Anna cried when she talked of first learning of her father's continued guilt. It obviously pained her to realize that her father thought he had ruined her life. Emily cried at remembering how much her daughter had suffered after the accident—seeing her laying in the hospital bed with tubes and needles sticking out of her, learning that she would never walk again, and watching her painful physical therapy. However, the most emotional by far was Gary. He started to cry before he could even squeak out the first word, and continued right through to the very end. And it can only be expected that when the father of the family carries on so, the rest of the household would feel inclined to join in. The entire Harmon clan, with the exception of Troy, who was currently proselyting in the northernmost regions of Venezuela, sat in a circle and cried.

Dr. Brooks opened a brand new box of Kleenex and started to pass them around. "Well, I think this was a pretty good start," he commented. "Shall we meet again at the same time in two weeks?"

"SO YOUR DAD really opened up and cried?"
"Yeah. My whole family did."
"I know, but your dad too?"

Anna sighed heavily into the phone. "Brian, there is nothing wrong with my dad crying. I thought it was great."

"Oh, Anna! I didn't mean anything bad! I think it's absolutely fantastic! It's very healthy to have a good cry. I wish my father would cry sometimes."

"Really? Oh . . . I'm sorry. I misunderstood you."

"Forget about it. So what else happened?"

"That's it. We each told our version of the story, then the tears started. We have another appointment in two weeks. Dr. Brooks didn't tell us what we would be doing, so I have no idea what to expect. But I'm sure whatever happens will be a step forward."

There was a brief pause in the conversation. Anna was about to speak again when Brian jumped in.

"Anna, I'm really happy that this is working out for your family. And I'm happy about something else, too."

Anna's heart immediately jumped into her throat. "Oh, really?" she asked, trying desperately to sound calm. "What else?" Her heart began to race and she mentally scolded herself for jumping to conclusions. *He is probably happy that we are friends, or that my mom drives him to school, or something dumb like that.*

"I am happy that you are going to the summer activity, and that we are riding in the same car. I think we will have fun together."

Aaahhh! Anna screamed wildly in her head. Her palms started to perspire, as did the back of her knees.

"I wouldn't have missed this trip for the world. I'm really looking forward to it."

"Sorry, Anna. Someone's trying to get through on the other line, and my mom is expecting a call from my aunt. I better go."

"Yeah, okay."

"I'll see you at school tomorrow, right?"

"Of course!"

"See ya, Anna."

"Bye, Brian."

CHAPTER 14

THE LAST seven days of school went by far too slowly for Anna. Ever since her phone conversation with Brian on Monday night, her head had been in the clouds and her stomach had been on the world's longest roller coaster. And every time she saw him, her condition worsened. And now she saw him more often than just in art class and on the way to and from school. They ate lunch together, went to the youth activity night together, and even sat together at church. Luckily for Anna, she did not have to suffer alone. Rebecca was quickly becoming just as mental about Karl. Yet, Karl appeared to be a little more obvious about his feelings for Rebecca than Brian had ever been about his feelings for Anna. Seeing Karl act goofy and say stupid things whenever Rebecca was around always gave Anna a sick, jealous feeling. What she wouldn't give to have Brian say one dumb thing to her, or even give her one cross-eyed glance! But he never lost control; he was always as cool as a cucumber.

Wednesday was the final day of school, and the youth advisors decided to throw a potluck dinner and dance for all the youth. Of course, all of the kids were abuzz with excitement—everyone except Anna, that is.

Why did they have to plan a stupid dance? she thought. Why couldn't they have just left it with a dinner? Things were going so well, and now it's all a mess! What am I going to do? If I stay home, Brian will go and have a great time with someone else. But if I go, I'll be forced to watch him dance without me. I guess I could show up for dinner, and then make up some excuse to leave before the dance starts. That way I'll get to spend time with him, and I'll be spared the misery of seeing him with other girls. Gosh! Why did they have to plan a stupid dance!

By the time Wednesday finally rolled around, Anna had everything planned. While she was getting dressed, she went over the conversation she would have with Connie and Rebecca. One of them, Connie no doubt, would tell her she should stay for the dance. Rebecca would throw in how fun it would be just to sit and listen to the music. Then Anna would drop her perfectly manicured story on both of them. She would explain how her father was so proud of her and Jason, and that he wanted to do something special for them. She could stay for dinner, but after that she would have to go home. Her father wanted it to be a surprise, so he wouldn't say what they were doing, just that it would be fun. Connie and Rebecca would have to buy that story; it was too good for them not to!

Four and a half hours later, the conversation in Anna's head occurred. However, it didn't go exactly as planned. It started out right, but it was not long before Anna lost control of the situation without realizing it. "Anna, you should stay for the dance tonight," Connie stated.

Anna looked over at Rebecca and waited for her to say her line, and that's when things went screwy.

"Yeah, Anna," Brian interjected. "Please stay for the dance. I've noticed you never come to them, and I think we would have a great time. I know the guy playing the music, and he'll play anything that you want to hear. Will you please stay with me . . . uh, us?"

Anna was completely flabbergasted. Her chin was practically resting in her lap. She cleared her throat and looked at Connie, who for the first time ever was thoroughly speechless. Anna then looked back at Brian, who was still waiting for an answer.

"Well, I . . . uh," she paused, "I guess since I'll already be there, I could stay for . . . a few songs." *A few songs?!* she thought. *What the heck am I saying? Did I really just tell him I'd stay tonight? What happened to my plan? It was foolproof! I guess foolproof doesn't necessarily mean Brian-proof!*

"Oh, good! We'll have fun, you'll see!"

Connie still hadn't found her voice. She continued to stare at Anna as if she had suddenly sprouted a second head.

Yeah, the dance should be really great, Anna thought.

CHAPTER 15

Thursday, June 19

Dear Diary,

I know I start every entry the same way, but this time I mean it more than ever before: you're not going to believe what happened! It seems like my life has been changing by leaps and bounds over the last month or so. I resisted the change at first. I was quite happy with how my life was, and I wasn't looking for changes. But now that so many things have taken place, I am thrilled!

The most recent event took place just last night. Yesterday was the last day of school, and there was a dinner and dance for the youth. I had prepared my excuse for when Connie and Rebecca. But I was ambushed from behind! It wasn't Connie and Rebecca hounding me, it was Connie and Brian! I guess Becca was too busy making googly eyes with Karl. When Brian asked me to stay for the dance, I folded like a house of cards. At this point if Brian asked me to eat a big, hairy bug, I'd probably do it.

The dinner part went just as I thought it would. I have been to plenty of those to know how they work. But I started to get really nervous when the tables were being pushed to the side to clear a dance floor. I had never been to a dance before, but I had imagined what they would be like. I pictured everyone jumping up to dance with every song, and I would spend the night sitting alone in a corner. But you know what? They are nothing like that! None of the younger *girls ever really danced, they were too busy running to the bathroom. And the ones that did dance, well, let's just say that it wasn't every song. In fact, I was never completely alone the entire night. It was really a lot of fun. We talked, sang, and watched everyone jump around. Becca and Karl were lost in their own world. Connie danced with a few different guys, but no one that made her palms sweat. But the most wonderful part was that Brian only danced twice, once with Connie and once with dumb old Sarah Garth. But he only danced with her because she asked him, and Brian is too nice to say no. He spent the rest of the night with me at the table. He asked me to dance a couple of times, and one was even a slow dance. But I said no. I would have been too embarrassed to just sit there and snap my fingers. He said he understood and he would wait until I felt more comfortable, no matter how long it took. It would have been a really great moment, except that's when dumb old Sarah showed up.*

    I had a pretty cool time, and I'm actually thinking about going to the next one. I know it will be different, because tonight was just our ward. At the regular dance more people show up. I don't know, maybe I won't go. I have two weeks to decide.

    Oh, yeah. SCHOOL'S OUT!!!

The Church is true . . .
Anna

CHAPTER 16

"Emily, I've been thinking. And the more I think about it, the less I like it."

Emily and Gary Harmon were sitting together in the family room. The television was playing a rerun of an old Perry Mason episode, but both Emily and Gary weren't paying much attention to it.

"Did you hear me, Emily?"

She put down her book and looked at her husband impatiently. "I heard you, Gary," she sighed. "I was just waiting for you to tell me what the heck you are talking about."

"I'm talking about this Disneyland trip. I know I agreed to it before, but now I'm not so sure."

Emily dismissed him with a sigh and went back to her book.

"No, really, Emily. I think we need to talk about this some more. Please listen to me."

"Yes, my love, I am listening to you," Emily replied without looking up from what she was doing.

"Emily, I don't like the idea of Anna traveling all the way to Los Angeles. I mean, what if something happens? I wouldn't be able to get there for a couple of hours. Six, if I had to drive!"

Now she did look up at him. "Have you forgotten that I will be there with her? You sound as if you don't trust me to handle a problem situation. And quite frankly, that offends me."

"There's no need to get angry. You know very well that's not what I meant at all. I just meant that it makes me nervous to have her so far away—to have both of you so far away."

"Would it make you feel any better if I promised to call and check in every day?"

Gary sighed and thought it over. "Yeah, I do want you to call. But I also want you to realize that I am going to worry every second of every day."

Emily smiled and patted her husband's arm. "Gary, that's only natural! Of course you're going to worry, but don't misinterpret your feelings."

"What do you mean? Misinterpret them how?"

Emily laughed at the look on her husband's face. "What I mean is that you should worry about your daughter, not your daughter in the wheelchair! Don't you think that every parent is going to worry about their child during the trip? But Gary, just because we worry doesn't mean we should lock her in her bedroom her whole life. I believe the most important thing we can do for her is give her the chance to be independent and mingle with her friends for a week. Think about it! You've always said that your biggest heartache was that she could never do normal teenage activities. Well, here is her chance, and you don't want to let her go!"

Gary sat silent throughout her whole argument, staring down at his hands. When Emily finally stopped talking, she noticed that a tear trickled slowly down his cheek.

"Oh, Gary! What is wrong? Please don't cry."

"You are right," he choked, "right about everything. She does need her independence. I just wanted to be there to protect her from ever being hurt again."

"Those are also normal feelings. Every father wants to protect his daughter from being hurt, wheelchair or no wheelchair. It's a fact of life. We just have to make sure that we don't cut her off from the rest of the world merely because she can't walk."

Gary brushed away a second tear that had started its long journey down his face. "How did you get to be so smart?"

Emily laid her head on Gary's shoulder. "Living with you, my dear. Now hush, Perry is about to tell us who did it."

CHAPTER 17

"WHAT DO you mean you were almost not going to Disneyland?!" Connie demanded. She had been looking at a turquoise t-shirt that was on the sale table in front of The Gap. She dropped it immediately and whipped around to face Anna, her eyes as big as saucers.

"Oh, it's all okay. I'm going again."

"Well, tell us what happened! Did you change your mind or something?" Rebecca asked.

"I bet she just got nervous at the thought of Brian seeing her in shorts!" Connie teased. She turned back to the table and started to re-examine the t-shirt.

"If you really want to know, I overheard my dad talking to my mom in the living room yesterday. He said that he was worried about me going so far away."

"My dad isn't exactly thrilled about it either," Connie said over her shoulder. "But he would never dream of telling me that I had to stay home. He knows how much I really want to go." Rebecca joined Connie at the sales table. "I'm glad you are still going, Anna. It wouldn't be the same without you."

"Well, you can thank my dear, old mom. She's the reason I'm going."

"All right! Score one for Momsie! What'd she do? Strong arm him a little? Maybe some Indian wrestling?" Connie asked as she left the sale table and headed for the nearest rack.

"Yeah! How did you know?" Anna laughed. "I almost blew my spy cover to rescue the poor guy!"

"Oh, Anna, that's so sweet," Rebecca cooed. "He was worried about his only daughter."

"Actually," Anna replied matter of factly, "he was worried about his only daughter who is in a wheelchair. He wouldn't have had the same feelings if I could walk."

The smile on Rebecca's face quickly faded. Connie stopped her search for the perfect shirt. She knelt down beside Anna's chair.

"Why would you think that? Is that what your dad said?"

Anna shrugged her shoulders. "Basically. My mom told him he was confused, or something like that. I couldn't really hear it all, but I think my dad was crying. Anyway, my mom somehow got him to see that it would be okay for me to go."

Rebecca's chin began to wobble and she appeared to be on the verge of tears. "Gosh, Anna, I'm sure it's not really what you think. Besides, there's nothing wrong with a father worrying about his daughter, chair or no chair."

"I know. But it still hurts a little to know that my dad thinks of me as his daughter in a wheelchair."

The three girls sat silent for a moment, each feeling extremely awkward. But not to anyone's surprise, Connie broke the silence.

"I wish I had something even remotely intelligent to say that would make you feel better. I would even settle for something halfway stupid. But I'm drawing a blank. It sounds like a problem your family will have to work out together. Maybe your fancy therapist could start earning his fees and help you guys solve this."

"Hey, yeah, Anna! Just mention how you feel at your next session and let the doctor tell you what to do."

Anna shook her head vigorously. "Nothin' doin'! If I said anything, they would know I was eavesdropping. My dad would pop his cork!"

"Oh, yeah," Connie and Rebecca agreed simultaneously, then punched each other and yelled "Jinx!" They turned to Anna and pleaded with their eyes for her to say their names so they could speak again. Anna laughed at their dopey expressions, then folded her arms and pretended to contemplate which one to set free.

"By a show of hands, which one of you is so desperate for her voice that she is willing to buy me a chocolate chip cookie and a large Sprite?"

Both girls shot up their hands as fast as they could.

"And the winner is . . . Connie!"

"Oh, yes!" Connie yelled excitedly.

Rebecca frowned and kicked the front wheel of Anna's chair. Connie and Anna looked at each other and giggled.

"Should we?" Connie asked.

"Well . . . ," Anna started, then felt another jolt as Rebecca kicked her wheel again. "Okay, okay! I guess you can buy me some popcorn, R . . . R . . . Rebe . . ."

By now Rebecca was chomping at the bit and rocking from one foot to the other.

"R-R-R-Rebecca!"

Rebecca heaved a heavy sigh as if the weight of the world had been lifted off her chest. "You guys think you are so funny! Just wait till you're jinxed! I won't say your name until I get ten dollars!"

Connie and Anna screamed with laughter.

"Ha, ha," Rebecca sneered. "Come on, and I hope you choke on your popcorn."

CHAPTER 18

WHEN EVERYONE was finally seated and comfortable, Dr. Brooks stood up and walked around to the front of his desk. He picked up a chair and placed it against his desk so that whoever sat there would be facing the rest of the family.

"Now," he started, "last time we met, I asked each of you to write down a couple of questions for the other members of the family. We will treat this just like a Barbara Walters special—I want all questions asked and answered as directly and honestly as possible. But please remember that we are not doing this to accuse anyone of anything, nor do we want to hurt anyone's feelings. I will be listening carefully to each question asked, and if I feel one is inappropriate or spiteful I will ask you to move on. If everyone is ready, then we will start with Jason."

Jason looked up from his lap and scanned the room nervously. Emily reached over and gently rubbed his back.

"Go ahead, honey. It will be okay."

Jason slouched into his chair and slowly shook his head. "No, I don't want to go first. Make someone else go."

"Jason!" Gary called. "Get up there!"

"No, no, Mr. Harmon," Dr. Brooks responded immediately. "It's quite all right if Jason wants to wait for another turn. After all, this exercise won't work unless all participants are willing. Why don't we have Mrs. Harmon go first."

"Emily sucked in her breath; she suddenly knew exactly how Jason felt. "Very well." she sighed, trying desperately to sound calm. She stood up and walked over to the proverbial "hot seat." She unfolded the paper on which she had written her questions. She glanced over at Dr. Brooks. "I only have two questions."

"That is absolutely fine, Mrs. Harmon. Start whenever you are ready."

Emily drew air deep into her lungs and held it for a moment, then slowly let it out. It was a technique to get rid of butterflies that she had learned back in her high school drama class. She did it now without even realizing it.

"My first question is for Anna. Since the accident, have you ever once resented your father, and do you feel like your life is ruined?"

Gary looked at his wife in utter disbelief and then dropped his head in shame. He didn't dare look at his daughter.

"Oh, gosh no, Mom! I don't hate Dad, I love him! I always have, honest! I may not be so thrilled about what happened, but I don't hate Dad for it. I know that he didn't hurt me intentionally. Uh, what was the other part?"

"Do you feel that your life is ruined?" Emily repeated.

Anna thought for a moment. She looked over at her father. His face was a deep red, and he still wouldn't look up from his lap.

"No," she answered quietly. There was another brief pause.

"Would you like to say anything else, Anna?" Dr. Brooks asked.

"Well . . . I just don't know quite how to put it. I mean, it's obvious that my life has definitely changed. There are things I won't be able to do, no one can argue with that. But at the same time, there are still so many things I can do. My answer to your question, Mom, is no. My life is not ruined."

Mother and daughter exchanged brief glances, then both looked over at Gary Harmon. His face was completely buried in his hands. He sensed that all eyes were on him, so he pulled out his handkerchief and wiped his eyes. He got up from his chair and crossed the room to Anna. He knelt beside her chair and hugged her tightly.

"I love you so much, Anna. And I am so sorry." His tears were flowing again, and he made no attempt to hide them.

"I know, Dad. I love you, too."

He stroked her hair, then stood up to return to his chair.

"That's all I have." Emily's voice was barely audible.

"Didn't you have two questions?"

"Yes," she responded. "But I've decided that I don't want to ask the other one."

"Dr. Brooks reached up and massaged the back of his neck. "Well, that's fine, Emily. But please keep in mind that the situation can not be completely corrected until all unanswered questions have been brought out in the open."

She looked back down at the second question she had written. It was directed at Jason, and it also involved her husband. She looked at Gary, who seemed to know exactly what she was thinking.

"Go ahead," he whispered. "It needs to be asked."

She reread the question silently, then focused on her son. "Jason, knowing the pain and suffering your sister went through, would it really be worth it to have been injured just to receive a few gifts?"

Jason sighed heavily and rolled his eyes. "Well, gosh, Mom! You don't have to put it that way!"

"How would you prefer me to say it? You seem to believe that Anna's pain was worth a computer and exercise bike, and you wished for the same. I know that your sister would give it all back to be able to do the things that you can do."

Jason folded his arms angrily over his chest and slumped deeper in to his chair. "Is it such a crime to want some attention from Dad?"

"No, son, it isn't. I just wanted you to know that you don't have to be injured to get that attention. Your father loves you very much, and he doesn't want to see you get hurt."

Jason looked at his father, who nodded in agreement. "I don't really want to be in a wheelchair, Mom. I just don't understand why we can't afford my pitching net, but we can afford Anna's bike."

"I know, Jason. And your father realizes his mistake, too. That's why we are here." Emily stood up and walked back to her seat. "That's really all I have, Dr. Brooks."

"That was excellent—exactly how I hoped it would work. Would you like to try your questions now, Jason?"

"I could only think of one," Jason responded as he reached in his back pocket.

"Quite all right. Come on up."

Jason did as he was told. When he was seated he unfolded the paper and looked up at his family. "This is for whoever wants to answer it. Does this mean that Anna will be giving back all the stuff Dad gave her?"

"Jason!" Gary snapped.

"It's a fair question, Mr. Harmon. It's obvious that he resents all the presents Anna received. It's a subject he needs to talk about. Go ahead, Jason."

"Thank you, Dr. Brooks," Jason quipped a little sarcastically. "Well? Does she have to give them back?"

Gary cleared his throat. "Only if she wants to, Jason. But I am not going to demand them back, just as I would never demand back any gift from you."

Jason sat for a moment considering his father's response. He looked up at Dr. Brooks. "Can I ask another question that I just thought of?"

"Absolutely, you may."

When Jason switched his gaze to Anna, she knew exactly what he was going to say. "Anna, are you gonna give anything back?"

She couldn't help but smile, and even found herself trying to suppress a giggle. "I knew you were going to ask me that, runt. And for your information, I had already decided on what to do long before today." Anna turned to look at her father. "Dad, I want to give back the exercise bike."

"But, Anna . . .," he protested.

She held up her hand to silence him. "Please, listen. The idea is great, and I really appreciate the thought. But I don't need an expensive bike when I can only use half of it. If we return it, we can get me some little dumbbells and wrist weights. Then we can use the extra money to buy Jason a pitching net."

"Yeah!" Jason added excitedly.

"Are you sure, Anna? Is that really what you want to do?"

"Yes, Dad. I'm positive. We can take the bike back tomorrow."

"Well," Gary looked to his wife, who could only shrug. "I guess if it's what you want, I'll take it back tomorrow."

"Yahoo!" Jason shouted. He jumped up and danced his way back to his seat.

Emily leaned over and hugged her daughter around the shoulders. "That was a wonderful gesture, Anna. I am so proud of you. Jason, don't you have something to say to your sister?"

"Thank you, Anna! Thank you, thank you!"

"You're welcome, squirt."

Dr. Brooks moved the "hot seat," allowing Anna to roll her chair into position. She hadn't bothered to write her question down. She knew exactly what she wanted to ask.

"I only have one question, too. I want to know why I'm no longer Dad's daughter, but Dad's daughter in a wheelchair."

Jason gasped. Gary's hands flew up to cover his mouth. Emily's eyes grew into large saucers, and all the color drained from her face. The only person who didn't react was Dr. Brooks.

"Anna," Emily whispered hoarsely. "What on earth put such an idea into your head?"

"You did, Mom."

"From me? What do you mean?"

Anna opened her mouth to speak, then closed it again. *Am I stupid?* she wondered. *Tell them I was listening around the corner? I'll be royally busted! But what am I going to do—lie about it? Out of the question.* "I, uh, . . . overheard you and Dad talking last week about the Disneyland trip."

Gary and Emily looked stupidly at each other. Anna had braced herself for the unbridled wrath of her parents, but as the seconds ticked by without an eruption, she slowly eased up. Her parents could only sit gape-mouthed. Anna thought a verbal onslaught would be bad, but their silence was murder.

"I know I shouldn't have been listening," she continued, "but when I heard Disneyland mentioned, I couldn't help myself."

"Did you hear the entire conversation, Anna?" Emily finally spoke up.

"Most of it. Why?"

"Because I addressed that specific topic with your father."

Anna felt a flush rising in her face. She suddenly decided it was a huge mistake bringing up the subject, and she silently put a curse on Connie for talking her into it. Her throat had gone completely dry, and it clicked when she swallowed. "What was his reason?"

Gary put his hand on Emily's arm. "I think I should answer this one, honey." Emily smiled and leaned back in her chair.

"Anna, I know it must have hurt you deeply when you heard us talking. And I want you to know that ever since that day I have tried very hard to change my way of thinking. I won't insult you by making up some wonderful excuse to rationalize my behavior. I was completely wrong, and I admit it. I wanted to protect you from, well, everything. I never want to see you hurt again, Anna. I know I went overboard, and I'm sorry. I really want to change, but you'll have to be patient with me. I can't do it overnight. You are my beautiful daughter, and I love you. Will you please forgive me?"

"Oh, Daddy!" Anna's voice trembled as she began to cry. She held out her arms to him, and he rushed to embrace her. Looking at her husband and daughter this way, Emily's heart swelled with joy.

When Gary finally stood up, he pushed her back to her spot while Dr. Brooks replaced the "hot seat." "I guess it's my turn," Gary commented as he sat down. "I have three questions, one for each of you. It's the same question, but I need each of you to answer it honestly. We all know the accident was my fault. I should never have insisted on driving after taking those cold pills. What I need to know is . . . can you ever forgive me?"

He looked first to his wife. "Yes, Gary," she whispered. "I forgive you completely. I know that you are sorry for what happened."

"Thank you, honey." He looked at his daughter next. "Anna?"

"I already told you I forgave you, Dad. It was an accident. I know you would never purposely hurt any of us."

"That's right, sweetheart. I wouldn't." Lastly he looked to Jason. "Son? Do you forgive me? And not just for the accident, but for how I've made you feel since the accident?"

"I don't know, Dad."

"Jason!"

"No, Emily. It's okay. He's just being honest with me. Son, what are you unsure of?"

Jason folded his arms and shrugged. "I don't know. I mean, I know you didn't cause the crash on purpose, so I forgive you for that. But I still feel weird about all that other stuff."

"I totally understand. You need to see me change, not just hear me say it."

Jason shrugged again. "Yeah, I guess that's it. Are you mad?"

"Oh, heavens no! I respect your answer very much, and I think that you are being very mature about the whole situation."

Jason beamed at this.

"And I promise you, Jason, I'll start paying you so much attention that you'll beg me to leave you alone!"

The tension in the room lifted instantly, and everyone laughed.

"Okay, Dad," Jason squealed. "You're on!"

CHAPTER 19

ANNA and Connie were at the dining room table dropping spoonfuls of chocolate chip cookie dough onto baking sheets. Brian and Jason sat cross-legged on the family room floor playing video games. And Rebecca and Karl were snuggled close together on the couch, secretly holding hands between his leg and hers.

"So, you could have asked any question you wanted?" Connie asked as she popped a chocolate chip into her mouth.

"Yep. Just as long as it wasn't malicious or hurtful."

"And you really asked what I told you to ask?"

"Yes, I did, Connie. And you're lucky it turned out the way it did or I would have boxed your ears!"

Connie laughed as another chocolate chip disappeared into her mouth. "I know what I would have asked!" she stated enthusiastically. "I want to know why every time you take that first big swig of soda pop, you always have that blasted hiccup right after you swallow!"

"Yeah," Brian laughed, "and I want to know why girls always have to go to the bathroom together!" Karl snickered and was immediately punched in the shoulder.

"We don't!" Anna protested. "Besides, you never know what kind of weirdo is lurking around those stalls. It's for our own protection."

"Yeah!" Connie and Rebecca agreed unanimously.

Brian dropped the video controller and put his hands in the air. "Okay! Okay! I give! It was just a question!" He flashed Anna a smile that made her insides melt.

"I have a question," Rebecca spoke up. "Why do professional athletes wait until they are on camera to spit?"

"They're just trying to make their mommies proud!" Karl laughed.

Connie picked up the baking sheets and walked across the kitchen to the oven. "I know I would be proud to see my son spitting on national television," she replied tartly while carefully placing the cookies in to bake.

Anna giggled uncontrollably. "You guys are way off the deep end," she said, wiping her eyes. "How did we get here from talking about my therapy?"

"Our therapy!" Jason yelled.

"Right, right. Our therapy. Sorry to leave you out, runt."

"I'm not a runt, and I want some cookies."

"Jason, you know we're making these for our trip to Los Angeles! Go ask Mom to make you some."

Connie clucked her tongue. "Oh, Anna, just give him one. But make sure you take it from Bec's share."

"Hey!" Rebecca cried. "Don't take mine! Take Brian's!"

Brian looked up at her surprised, and his warship was promptly destroyed by a flying missile.

"Ha, ha, Brian! I win!" Jason declared with glee.

"Yeah, you did, little bud. Now I should go help your sister since she is making cookies for me."

Anna was staring at him, and when he met her gaze she dropped her eyes quickly.

"C'mon, Brian," Jason pleaded. "Just one more game. Please?"

"I'll play you, squirt." Karl jumped up from the couch and joined Jason on the floor. Naturally this meant that he had to let go of Rebecca's hand. And from the look on her face, this did not please her.

Brian joined Anna and Connie at the table. He picked up two spoons and scooped up some dough. Anna pushed her baking sheet closer to him, and he smiled another mind-boggling smile.

"These cookies smell great. You guys have done a really good job."

"Gee, thanks Bri-Bri!" Connie chuckled. "We were debating on whether or not to challenge Mrs. Fields for her throne, and now you've helped us decide. Anna, we're definitely going for it."

Brian rolled his eyes. "Please, Anna. Promise me you will never go into business with this woman. She's a lunatic!"

Anna smiled and patted Connie's arm. "Well, Con, I guess you'll have to find yourself another sucker, uh . . . business partner." Brian threw his head back and laughed, and Anna thought her heart would burst. Connie grinned and got up to check the cookies in the oven.

"When am I going to get my cookies?!" Jason hollered over his shoulder, never taking his eyes off the television screen.

"Jason!" Anna scolded. "Show some manners! At least say please."

"Pleeeeease?"

Connie pulled two cookies off the sheet she had just taken from the oven and put them on a paper towel. She put them down next to Jason, warning him that they were still hot. On her way back to the table, she noticed Anna giving her eye signals, so she made a bee-line for the couch instead.

Maybe this was a mistake, Anna thought with a sudden feeling of dread. *Now I have to talk to him! And not just any old topic will do. I have to be interesting and witty!* "So, um, are you excited about our trip?" *Excited about our trip? Did I say excited about our trip?! Gee, I don't think it gets any wittier than that!*

"Yeah, sure I am! In four days we'll be at Disneyland! We'll have a great time, but there's something I really want to do before we go."

Anna looked at him with eyebrows cocked. "Oh, really? Like what?"

"Uh, what time will your parents be home?"

Now Anna's interest was piqued. She leaned forward a little. "My parents? What do you want them for?"

"Never mind," Brian said coyly. "Just tell me when they'll be home."

"Well, I guess any time. They went to the post office to mail a package to Troy."

"Oh, hey! How is old Troy? Baptizing lots of people?"

Anna grinned at him. "Nice try. What do you want with my parents?"

Brian leaned back in his chair and locked his fingers behind his head. "Sorry, Charlie. You'll just have to wait until they come home."

From that moment until her parents got home fifteen minutes later, Anna never stopped questioning him. She tried everything she could think of, including bribing him with cookies and money. But Brian stood his ground and kept his mouth shut.

As soon as they heard her parents pull into the driveway, both Brian and Anna raced into the hallway to meet them.

"Hey!" Connie yelled. "What's going on?"

"Just stay there!" Brian yelled back. "We'll be back in a minute!"

When Gary and Emily Harmon came in the front door, they were immediately ushered into the living room.

"Anna, what's going on here?" Gary asked as he plopped into the overstuffed easy chair.

"I don't know, Dad. Brian wants to talk to you guys."

Emily had an amused look on her face. "What do you need, Brian?" she asked.

He cleared his throat and looked from Anna to her parents. Suddenly he seemed more nervous than Anna had ever seen him be. He sat down on a footstool near where Anna had parked her chair. He swallowed hard and looked at Anna.

"I would like permission to take Anna to the movies tomorrow night. Please."

Anna's eyes grew wide and her heart skipped a beat. A smile spread slowly across her lips. Her wildest dreams were coming true, and all she could do was grin like an idiot. She quickly looked at her mom and pleaded with her eyes to allow her to go. Gary and Emily looked at each other, probably waiting for the other to make the decision. After a brief, but painfully strained pause, Gary Harmon took control of the moment.

"Well, Brian, I don't know. After all, you're both only sixteen. You know the Church frowns on single dating before age eighteen."

"Oh, yes, I know, Brother Harmon. But this will be a group date. You see, Karl will be taking Rebecca, and Jim Walker from the ward has agreed to ask Connie."

Anna and Emily exchanged fascinated glances while Brian continued. "And I promise Brother Harmon, there will be no pairing off."

This remark took Gary completely by surprise, and he tried desperately to hide his smile. He looked to his wife for help, but found none there. He made a mental note to get her back for hanging him out to dry.

"Well," he started, searching desperately for something to say, "have you, uh . . . have you considered everything?"

The confused look on Brian's face prompted him to continue. "Her chair, for instance?"

"Dad, if you're worried about him lifting me in and out of it, you'll remember that he had plenty of practice when Mom was driving him to school." She shyly glanced over at Brian and found him beaming at her. She returned his smile and dropped her gaze.

There was another pause which ended with Emily nudging Gary and nodding her head. Gary looked at his beautiful daughter, who was once again pleading with her eyes for permission. He then looked at Brian, wondering who this boy was. Sure, he'd been over to visit with Anna quite a few times. But before that he had only seen him at church. Could he really trust his only daughter with this boy?

"Well," Gary started.

"Please, Daddy?" Anna asked, barely above a whisper.

"Go ahead, Gary," Emily prodded.

"I guess if your mother thinks it will be okay . . ."

"Oh, thank you, Dad!" Anna cried, clapping her hands together.

Brian got to his feet and shook Gary's hand. "Thank you, Brother Harmon. I promise I'll take good care of her."

Emily had to laugh out loud at this. "My goodness, you all are acting as if we gave you permission to be married!"

"Mom!" Anna squealed and blushed deeply.

"I know it's just a movie, Sister Harmon. But it means a lot that you trust me with your daughter."

"I'm glad you take this as a serious decision, young man," Gary responded in his most fatherly tone. "It makes me feel better about letting her go."

Brian shook his hand again, then got behind Anna's chair to push her back into the kitchen.

"Anna!" Connie hollered. "Time for more cookies!?"

"So, Brian," Emily chuckled. "You really have a date for Connie?"

"Yeah! And it wasn't as hard as I thought it would be. Jim agreed right away."

"You know, I meant to say something when you mentioned his name before."

Good old mom, Anna thought. Always the worry wart.

"I've never heard of him. Is he new in the ward?"

"Yeah, his family just moved here from Phoenix."

"Oh." Emily sounded a little concerned. "Don't they always film that show *Cops* in Phoenix?"

"Sometimes, Mom. But they are in Boston a lot more."

"Has Jim actually met Connie yet?" Gary asked a little sarcastically.

"He's seen her at church, but they haven't officially met."

"Well," Gary sighed, "that would explain a lot."

CHAPTER 20

BRIAN said he would be there to pick her up by 6:30 P.M., but by 5:30 Anna had all but changed her mind. She still wanted desperately to go out with Brian; she hadn't changed her mind about that. It was this movie thing. She had only gone to the movies with her family since the accident. She felt secure knowing her father was close by. Tonight her father wouldn't be there. Tonight it would just be her and Brian, and the other two couples of course. She didn't dare tell her apprehensions to her parents, because they would probably try to talk her out of going. So she just kept her mouth shut and continued to get ready for her first date.

Anna looked at the clock by her bed and panicked. Only one hour to go before the man of her dreams would be here to sweep her away! She quickly changed her blouse for the third time.

No, this one is not quite right either! she thought. *I need a power blouse—one that says, "Sure I'm a great date, but just wait until you see me as your wife!"*

Anna rummaged through her closet again, hoping to find that a new blouse had suddenly materialized.

What in the world am I . . . wait a minute. Of course! Mom's new teal colored blouse! It's cool enough that it just might work.

Anna rolled down the hallway and bellowed, "Mom!"

Anna looked in her dresser mirror. The blouse looked great; it made the statement she hoped it would. But now her hair ribbon and eye shadow clashed. She pulled the ribbon from her hair and searched her top drawer for a better match. She didn't have a teal one, but the white would do just fine. Now what to do about her eyes? She grabbed a Kleenex, spit on it, and vigorously wiped off the old color.

Teal shadow will make me look cheap, so I better stick with a nice neutral peach.

"Anna, Brian's here."

"Oh, no, Mom! I'm not ready yet!" She quickly applied the shadow on the other eye.

"Relax, honey. No woman is ever ready when her date arrives. I think it's a law or something."

Anna laughed and relaxed a little. She felt a slight throbbing in her jaw and realized that her teeth had been clenched. She put on her gold hoop earrings, which were just big enough to be daring, and turned her chair around to face her mother. "How do I look? Will he drop dead?"

"You look fantastic, honey. And I want to tell you how proud I am of you. And you're growing up . . . just so fast!"

Anna rolled her eyes at her mother's knack for sappiness. "Mom, it's just a group date. It's not a real date yet. You have another year before you need to turn on the water works."

"Just give me my moment, please. Besides, it is a real date. It's just not an exclusive one. Now let's go, I think we've kept him waiting long enough."

Emily pushed her daughter down the hallway and into the living room where Brian was waiting.

Oh, wow! Anna thought. *He's wearing that great khaki shirt that makes him look so tan. I could scream!*

"Hi, Anna. You look really pretty."

Anna blushed and quickly looked down at her lap. "Thank you. You look nice, too." She looked up without raising her head. Brian was still looking directly at her, and he was grinning widely.

"Are you ready to go? My mom needs the car so she can visit her sister tonight, so she's going to drop us off. Is that all right?"

Anna nodded and reached for her purse on the coffee table.

"I'll take it from here, Sister Harmon." Brian took hold of the chair's handgrips and pushed her towards the front door. Emily's concern was showing on her face. She opened the front door and watched Brian push her daughter out of the house and down the ramp Gary had built after the accident.

"Do you need any help, Brian?"

"No, thanks, Sister Harmon. We'll be just fine."

Emily stood on the porch, feeling utterly helpless as she watched Brian prepare to lift Anna into the Dailey's station wagon. He locked her wheels, removed the left armrest, then swooped her up in his arms with the agility only a young man could possess.

Emily had to admit that he didn't need her help. Brian carefully placed Anna in the backseat of the car, then began the tedious process of collapsing her chair. Emily watched him struggle for a few seconds before he learned the trick and folded it up. A couple more seconds and they were off, with Anna waving out the window.

As she turned to walk back into the house, Emily caught a glance of her husband peeking out the window. The setting sun was just bright enough to glisten off his tears.

"HOW ARE YOU doing this evening, Anna?"

"I'm fine, Sister Dailey. How are you?"

"I'm doing fine, dear."

The three of them rode in silence for about five blocks. They would be at Karl's house in a few minutes, and Anna knew she needed to say something while they were still alone.

How should I put it, though? How do I say it? Anna cleared her throat, leaned over, and whispered, "Brian?"

"What?" he whispered back.

"I have something to tell you, but I'm not sure how."

"What is it, Anna? Have you changed your mind about tonight?"

"Oh, gosh no, Brian. I'm . . . really happy to be here with you." Anna sneaked a peek at the rearview mirror to make sure his mother was not being a silent participant in their conversation.

"I've only been to the movies with my family since the accident. My dad was always there to make sure nothing happened. I'm just really nervous about being there without him."

Brian sat quietly, thinking about what she said. That was quite possibly one of his best qualities: he always took her concerns seriously and never made fun of them.

"What are you afraid might happen?"

"Oh, I don't know. What if my wheels come unlocked and I go screaming down the aisle?"

Brian waited for Anna to smile before laughing at her joke. "Well, Anna, I can think of one way to prevent that from happening."

"Oh, yeah? How? Put your bike lock on my wheels?"

"No. I could carry you into the theater and put you in a regular seat, then carry you out again when the movie is over."

Anna started to giggle, but stopped short when she saw the serious look on his face. "You're joking, aren't you?" *Please! Let him be joking!*

"No, I'm not. And actually, the more I think about it the better I like it. You know those movie theater seats are pretty low. If you were in your chair you would be towering over us. This way you will be closer."

Anna sucked in her breath and held it. Her stomach was a thousand knots. *He wants me to be close to him! Oh, I feel like I'm going to throw up!*

"Anna? What do you think?"

She studied his face. She didn't know what to think! She figured that he would make some sort of suggestion, but she thought it would be to change their plans! Maybe go for ice cream or something. But to carry her into the theater?

"What would we do with my chair?" *I can't believe I am even considering this!*

"Well, we won't need it at all in the theater, so we could leave it here in the car. And even if we decide to get a bite to eat after the movie, my mom will have to drive us anyway, so your chair will be here."

Anna could only look at him, her mouth hanging open. *Sure, this sounds really good in theory, but I just know something will go wrong.*

"Anna? What do you say?"

"Uh . . ." *Should I? Shouldn't I?* "I don't know, Brian. I would be really embarrassed."

"I'll be very careful, and we'll just go right in and right out. I promise not to hang around and flaunt you." Brian put on his most charming smile, and Anna couldn't help but smile back.

"Okay, if we do this you will have to promise me something."

"Sure! What?"

"You have to promise that my parents will never hear about it. My mom especially, she would just flip!"

"Hey! No problem! I can keep a secret."

Anna cocked her head towards his mother. "She'll know. And so will everyone on the date tonight."

Brian looked at the back of his mother's head. "Oh, yeah. Hmm. Well, I'll just have to talk to all of them and make them see how good the idea really is!"

Both Brian and Anna kept their mouths shut until everyone had been picked up. Then, just as he had promised, Brian divulged his plans to the rests of the group. Naturally, he encountered great opposition, especially from his mother. But after an intense discussion and several promises to be careful, even she agreed to keep the secret.

Sister Dailey pulled up in front of the box office, and four people jumped out of the car. One of his mother's stipulations was that Karl buy Brian and Anna's tickets. She absolutely refused to allow Brian to carry her while they stood in line.

Five minutes later, Karl reappeared with their tickets.

"Are you ready, Anna?"

She took a deep breath and looked out the window at the crowd. "I suppose so."

Brian got out of the car and crossed to her side. With her door open, he bent to pick her up. One arm slid under her legs, the other arm went around her back. When Anna's arms were locked securely around his neck, she braced herself to be lifted from the seat. But for some reason, Brian paused, then pulled away.

"What's wrong?" she asked.

"Anna," Brian sighed, "could you take off your seatbelt this time?"

She looked down, and sure enough, her seatbelt was still fastened. "Oops."

Once again Brian reached in the car for Anna, but this time he scooped her up as deftly as he had back at her house. Without even looking, Anna knew that all eyes were on them. She tightened her grip around his neck as they approached the ticket agent at the front door.

"He has our tickets," Brian announced, motioning to Karl with his head. The look on the ticket agent's face presented Karl an opportunity that he couldn't resist.

"They are newlyweds," Karl stated simply as he handed over the tickets. "He has vowed to carry her over every threshold for their entire first year of marriage."

Connie and Rebecca started to giggle and had to be propelled forward by their dates.

"Would you like anything to snack on, Anna?"

She smiled and looked around the lobby. "If you don't mind, why don't we find our seats first? Then you can come back out here."

Brian snickered. "Yeah, I guess that would be a wise decision."

They found the perfect row that would suit everyone, not too close for Connie and not too far for Rebecca. Brian set Anna down on the aisle seat, and then the three guys disappeared to get munchies.

"Okay, we don't have long before they come back," Connie whispered. "So spill it, Anna. Whose idea was it for Brian to carry you around all night?"

"It was his, really!"

Both Connie and Rebecca rolled their eyes and shook their heads. "We're not buying it," Rebecca retorted. "And I don't think anything you can say will change our minds."

"Well, believe what you want, I don't care." Anna replied quite coyly. "So now let's talk about Connie. That Jim is pretty cute!"

Connie's eyes were suddenly full of stars. "Yeah, he is, isn't he?" She giggled.

"Uh-oh, Anna," Rebecca laughed. "She's gone!"

"If you gotta go, there's no better way," Connie sighed dreamily.

Anna leaned back in her chair and folded her arms. "Isn't this great? By the end of summer, we might all have boyfriends!" They all exchanged lovesick glances and then burst into hysterics.

"What's so funny?" Brian asked.

Gasps were heard all around as the girls looked up to find that their dates had returned.

"Just girl stuff," Connie answered. "You know, Easy Bake ovens, nail polish, clip-on earrings, stuff like that."

"You're a nut," Jim laughed as he stepped past Connie to his seat. Connie looked at her girlfriends and blushed.

When everyone was seated and had their correct snack, they settled into comfortable small talk until the theater darkened and the movie started.

Brian had bought a large tub of popcorn for them to share. Both made sure not to reach in while the other's hand was inside, because they knew that sparks would fly if their hands touched.

When they had devoured the popcorn, Brian leaned forward and put the tub on the floor. Anna watched him do this, and then watched him sit back up and lay his arm on the armrest that separated them. She was suddenly overcome with déjà vu. Her mind was drawn back to the fireside she had missed because she had stared at this same arm the whole time.

Now I suppose I'll miss this movie, Anna thought. But how stupid I am to obsess over an arm. . .

"Can I hold your hand?"

Anna snapped her head up to see that Brian had leaned closer to her and was apparently waiting for her answer. She felt as if a tornado had just whipped through her head and wiped out all memory of the English language. She just sat looking into his beautiful eyes.

"If you don't want to, I'll understand." Brian took his arm off the armrest and laid it in his lap.

"Oh, no!" Anna finally blurted out. "I mean, yes. I would like to hold your hand."

Brian started to beam. "Really?"

Anna smiled and gave Brian her hand. "Really."

Brian took her hand, and she was instantly impressed with how carefully he touched her. Their hands came to rest on the edge of her chair. The feeling of his fingers intertwined with hers made her heart race and gave her goosebumps all over. And for the hundredth time since she met Brian Dailey, her mind wandered to their wedding day. She went over every detail from the moment they entered the temple together until they left for the honeymoon. She never got further than that point; it was too embarrassing to think of Brian that way. And of course she had no idea what the temple would be like, so she relied on her imagination to fill in the blanks. But the reception was always the same, and it was fabulous. She had never shared this dream with a solitary person—she had never even written it in her journal. And now the dream seemed more real than it ever had before.

Neither of them moved an inch for the duration of the movie. They sat almost like mannequins, afraid to even look at each other. When the movie ended and the lights came up, they dropped hands immediately, as did Karl and Rebecca and Connie and Jim. After a few moments of discussion, they decided to head to the corner cafe.

"Karl, could you and Jim see if my mom is here?" Brian asked.

"Yeah, sure." He stood up and then motioned for Rebecca to come.

"I guess I'll go, too," she said, jumping to her feet.

"Yeah, me too," Connie added. She stood up next to Jim, who threw her a sly little wink.

Brian waited until they were all gone before turning back to Anna. "Thank you for holding my hand. It was really nice."

Anna blushed and looked away. "It was nice," she agreed.

"Uh, Anna?" Brian started. "Will you go . . ."

"Brian!" Karl yelled from the back of the theater.

Brian looked up a little startled.

"Let's go! Your mom is here!"

"Well, are you ready?" he asked, standing up.

No! she screamed in her head. *Finish your question! Will I go where? Out again? Steady? To Las Vegas and get married?? What??*

"Yeah, I guess I'm ready." She said softly.

He bent over and quickly hoisted her up into his arms. She loved the way his muscles flexed every time he held her.

Whatever his question is, the answer is definitely yes!

CHAPTER 21

SISTER DAILEY dropped off the other two couples first. And although she loved her friends dearly, Anna was grateful when she was alone with Brian again. He quickly grabbed her hand again, and she relished every second of it.

When they arrived at Anna's house, Brian set up her chair and brought it over to Anna's side of the car. He carefully placed her on the foam padded seat, unlocked the wheels, and pushed her up the walkway to the front porch.

"Thank you, Brian. I had a wonderful time tonight."

"So did I, Anna. Thank you for coming with me."

Five uncomfortable seconds lapsed without a word from either of them. They looked everywhere but at each other.

If he doesn't make a move soon, I think I'll scream! Anna thought wildly.

And then he did. He held up his hand for a friendly handshake.

This is not quite what I had in mind, she thought, as she lifted her hand to take his. He grasped her hand gently and pumped it up and down a few times. Then, all of a sudden and without warning, he was bending over, coming closer and closer to her face. Anna's brain went into automatic overload. Could it possibly be true? Was Brian about to kiss her? His face was now hovering directly above hers. She closed her eyes and waited for it to happen. And then she felt it. Brian was softly pressing his lips against her left cheek. Her eyes flew open in time to see Brian straighten up again.

Is that it? A kiss on the cheek?? We can do better than that, Brian! And before her brain could reason with her hands, Anna reached up and grabbed Brian by the front of his shirt. All her arm exercises apparently paid off, because she pulled him down to her. Before Brian had the time to react, Anna planted a kiss right on his mouth. She let him go and he straightened up, his hand covering his freshly kissed lips. When she realized what she had done, Anna gasped and turned a brilliant red. She sat in utter horror, waiting for him to yell and scream at her.

He slowly lowered his hand, shock still registering on his face. And then he smiled. Not just a small, pleasant grin, but a big, gaping, every tooth showing smile. Anna let out the breath she had been holding in.

"I, uh . . . will see you, uh . . . tomorrow," Brian stammered. He turned to go and tripped over the garden hose. He managed to catch himself, but still looked back at Anna. Anna let out a little giggle and then waved as he headed towards his car.

CHAPTER 22

Sunday, July 16

Dear Diary,

I kissed Brian. I have no idea where I got the nerve. I guess because Brian makes me feel so good about myself, I can do anything. So I did! After it happened, I wasn't sure how he would react. But he smiled and tripped over the garden hose, so I guess he liked it!
    Actually, let me change that. After what happened at church today, I know he liked it!
    After sacrament meeting, Brian walked me out to my car. We were talking about a bunch of different subjects, but mainly about our trip to Los Angeles. We leave tomorrow morning at 6 A.M., so I was asking him if he was all packed. He just stared at me like he didn't hear what I said, so I asked him again. I barely got out the last word when he blurted out, "Anna, will you go steady with me?" He totally caught me by surprise! I was chewing a piece of gum, and I sucked it into my throat and choked on it! I started coughing, and Brian had to pound me on the back. When I was finally able to control myself, he asked me again!
    I couldn't believe it! My dream man was asking me to go steady! It was fantastic! I said " yes," of course. I would have to be a total idiot not to. After I agreed, he kissed me again. But this time it was no cheek-job like last night.

This time he kissed me on the lips. Maybe he was afraid that I would yank him down by the shirt again! It's been almost six hours since Brian became my boyfriend! It is so weird!

I told my mom when we got home from church. Naturally she got all psycho. She got this bizarre idea that we would always try to sneak off and be alone on dates and stuff. She told me that maybe we should hold off until next year when we turn seventeen. It took me a long time, but I finally convinced her that we would only do the group date thing. We had no plans to sneak off into dark corners anywhere. She finally said we could stay together, but she said that we were too young to be exclusive, so I had to promise that our friends would always be with us. I don't have a problem with that at all, because I love being with my friends! And being together with Brian will only make it that much better!

I absolutely can't wait for this trip tomorrow! And I am glad that my mom is coming with me. It will be nice to spend time alone with her. It seems like whenever we are together, Jason is always there. This will be a nice change.

It's getting pretty late, and I still have to pack for tomorrow. I get butterflies every time I think about spending the week with Brian. I just know I'll say or do something stupid! I'll write again as soon as we get back.

The Church is true . . .
Anna

CHAPTER 23

ALL OF the youth started arriving at the church parking lot at 5:45 A.M. When Anna and Emily got there, Connie showed them their van. Brian was behind the van, helping load suitcases. As soon as he saw her, he gave his girlfriend a big smile and a wave.

By six the vans were all loaded and ready to go. The adults took a quick roll call, then Bishop Caldwell offered a prayer.

Parents and children bid their farewells. There were kisses, hugs, and promises to use sunscreen. The advisors controlled the chaos of loading kids in the correct cars as best they could. But when you are dealing with kids who are excited about a trip to Disneyland, this is no easy task.

Brian lifted Anna out of her chair and handed her up to Emily, who placed her on the bench seat of the van.

I love you, Mom," Anna whispered. "And I'm really glad you are coming along."

"I love you too, sweetheart," Emily whispered back, and kissed her daughter on the forehead.

After he helped everyone else get in, Brian climbed into the van. He plopped down next to Anna, fastened his seatbelt, leaned over and kissed her lightly on the cheek.

"You look really pretty this morning."

Anna blushed and elbowed him in the ribs. "Stop it," she giggled.

The vans and cars roared into life, and the convoy was on its way. As their van left the parking lot and headed for the highway, Brian grabbed Anna's hand and held it tightly. But this time he made no attempt to hide it.